———— ★ ————

I started back down the passenger side of the van, deciding to take out the jack and at least try to tackle the flat myself, aware of the sound of an engine first and that it was growing louder, separate from the freeway, a full-throated V-8 growl.

I glanced over. A big truck, an overgrown pickup with no lights, blasted down the perimeter road. Suddenly it veered into the parking area—trying to miss the speed bumps, I thought. And it would do that, all right.

Only one problem: huge as a locomotive, unswerving as destiny, the truck plunged straight at me.

———— ★ ————

"...brisk characterization and smooth plotting."
—*Publishers Weekly*

"Delilah's latest caper belongs in the must-read category."

—*Booklist*

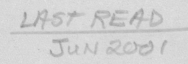

LAST READ

JUN 2001

Also available from Worldwide Mystery by
MAXINE O'CALLAGHAN

SET-UP

Maxine
O'Callaghan
Trade-Off

WORLDWIDE®

TORONTO • NEW YORK • LONDON
AMSTERDAM • PARIS • SYDNEY • HAMBURG
STOCKHOLM • ATHENS • TOKYO • MILAN
MADRID • WARSAW • BUDAPEST • AUCKLAND

TRADE-OFF

A Worldwide Mystery/February 1996

First published by St. Martin's Press, Incorporated.

ISBN 0-373-26191-8

I am extraordinarily blessed to count as longtime friends so many talented writers who give me both objective criticism and loyal support. This book is for three of them:
Don Stanwood, Kaye Klem and Jean Femling.

ONE

"EVER KILL ANYBODY, Ms. West?"

The clerk in the gun store had my permit so he knew my profession. A woman who makes her living as a PI ought to be used to the kind of sly eagerness for blood-and-guts details I heard in his voice. I'm not.

I said, "If you do the job right, you don't have to kill people."

"Yeah, but have you?"

"No."

"Sometimes I bet you'd like to," he said sagely. "Otherwise you wouldn't be looking at this."

This was a Beretta mini-automatic with a blue-steel finish and walnut grips. Ten shots—one in the chamber and nine in the magazine. Not much stopping power, but it would certainly slow a person down. The sneaky little piece was made for close-up work and could be tucked in a pocket or worn in a clip-on holster.

Theoretically this meant I would keep the gun on my person and have it handy when the bad guys showed up. I'd had a couple of experiences recently that convinced me I ought to be taking such precautions. And, yes, if I'd had such a weapon in my hands during those times, I would have put some neat little .22-caliber holes in a couple of very nasty people. However, I was not going to tell this guy about any of that.

He looked disappointed at my silence, said, "Well, you need some protection, this baby will certainly fill the bill. And nobody'll ever know you have it."

Sure.

The gun might be small, but only a moron would fail to discover it on a routine patdown.

"I'll take it," I said.

THE WAITING PERIOD for gun registrations in California is two weeks so twelve days later I didn't have the Beretta yet. Not that I expected to need it. I was driving down to south Orange County on a gorgeous September morning to meet with a client. It was the kind of day that made me long for a convertible or at least a sunroof in the Astro van. The skies were a brilliant, smogless blue, and the air smelled of drying grass and the mingled scent of unnamed flowers with just a hint of pungent eucalyptus.

To tell the truth I was having second thoughts about the mini-automatic. I skirted around any niggling doubts about really using it to best advantage and dwelt on the physical problems of concealment in the Southern California heat. Women's clothes are not designed to hide much of anything and seldom come with useful pockets. And I refuse to wear boots and an ankle holster.

Maybe, I told myself, I was overreacting. Sure, I'd had some close calls lately. Still, with enough caution a PI can spend an entire career in no more danger than if he or she had taken up accounting or strawberry farming.

I fervently intended to practice caution.

Like today. The man I was going to see lived in Nellie Gail Ranch, a medium-posh development for the horsy set in Laguna Hills. Benjamin Wylie wouldn't give me details over the phone, only that it was a personal matter. I hoped for some nice, nonviolent problem, maybe horse rustling, but in any case I reminded myself that I could always say a polite no thanks.

Simple.

Now if only I could shake the feeling that the dangerous ones track me down and sit on my doorstep like a homeless dog.

As if to underscore that feeling, when I turned into the development two huge black crows picked at a roadkill in the street, what looked like the fresh remains of a possum. The birds flapped away at the last moment before my approach, a slow, indifferent flight of accommodation rather than fear which brought them back to settle on their meal as soon as I had passed.

And in the sky an even bigger bird, quite possibly a buzzard, wheeled in lazy circles over the top of a hill, the one Wylie lived on, naturally.

I wished I'd insisted that he come to the office for the meeting. However, people with money just expect you to do whatever suits their convenience. I had some idea of Wylie's financial standing because his secretary had placed the call, announcing that Mr. Wylie of Pacifico Lighting was on the line. Easy enough to do a quick check after our conversation and learn that his company was solid, privately owned, and grossed $30 million last year by making inexpensive lamps and lighting fixtures, the kind you find in discount stores.

So here I was, appropriately dressed in a tan skirt and white silk blouse, panty hose, and heels. Well, actually, the brown pumps sat on the floor next to my new leather briefcase. I drove in an old pair of huaraches and wished for bare legs.

The street wound up through custom-built houses set on enough acreage for steep pastures where horses grazed behind split-rail fences. The houses were big and pretentious, leaning toward English Tudor and French colonial, some complete with turrets and mullioned windows. Moats, I presumed, were optional. Wylie's was about seven thousand square feet of Cuisinart architecture on a hilltop cul-de-sac. Two stories of red brick, shutters and dormers, a hip roof, and a Tara-style front entrance flanked by plantings of full-grown palms, birds of paradise, and long-needled pines in beds mulched with cinder-gray lava rock. It loomed over a smaller, one-story next door, this one a California ranch style that looked as though it had been built here by mistake.

I parked the van on Wylie's driveway, changed my shoes, and got out. Another crow flew past, the beating of its enormous, glossy wings sounding like small helicopter rotors, *whoop, whoop, whoop.* It lit on a pine, stared at me while I climbed the steps to Wylie's front door, then flapped off.

Maybe the bird was more properly called a raven. Whatever.

The damn thing gave me the creeps. If any aliens from outer space have managed to sneak in and take over life forms, I nominate these big birds as likely candidates. While I rang the doorbell, I caught a faint smell of something putrid, the buzzard's lunch I supposed, a gopher or a roof rat that had eaten poisoned bait and crawled off to die. The people who live here do not peacefully coexist with wild things.

A Latino woman answered the door. She wore a black cotton dress and black running shoes. Not exactly a uniform but close enough. Heavy dark hair was pulled back from the round face and secured with a clasp at the nape of her neck.

"I'm Delilah West," I said. "Mr. Wylie's expecting me."

She nodded, expressionless, and gestured me into a dimly lighted entry. Closing the massive front door deepened the gloom, which was a product of burgundy wallpaper and floors of a dark wood, walnut or maybe teak. I'd bet the woman had to dust-mop them twice a day.

As she led the way, I caught glimpses of various small, crowded rooms. The one where Benjamin Wylie waited had a wall of bookshelves and a desk with enough area for a fax machine and a computer. There was also an overstuffed couch and two chairs, plus a full complement of tables and heavy brass lamps that hadn't been made by Pacifico Lighting for sale at Kmart. Maybe this room and the others only seemed small because they were jammed with furniture.

The maid stopped, blocking the entry, and rapped on the open door. Wylie sat at the desk, reading some kind of bound reports in plastic covers.

"Well, don't just stand there, Elena," Wylie said and the woman moved aside. "Ms. West? Come in, please."

He stood up and came around the desk. Midfifties, I guessed. His stocky body was sturdy and compact in tailored navy slacks, a sportshirt in dark khaki accented with thin navy stripes. His thick hair was the color of iron filings and clipped short. Pale blue eyes studied me beneath brows that were a shade darker gray than his hair and needed tweezing or a trim.

I presume I met with his approval because he gestured and said, "Come and sit down. Elena, please bring some fresh coffee. Is that all right, Ms. West? Or would you prefer something else?"

"Coffee's fine."

I took one of the chairs; he sat across from me on the sofa. More of the dark wood floors in here and the furniture was all a deep forest green. Through French doors I could see a patio with pots of flowers and beyond that the glimmer of a pool, but the sunny world outside seemed strangely subdued.

Tinted glass in the windows, I realized. And I'd bet they were never opened to let in a balmy breeze. The air in the room was chill and stale.

Once we were settled, I said, "Tell me what I can do for you, Mr. Wylie."

"It's my daughter, Tamra."

He glanced over at a silver-framed photo on an end table. In the picture he held a chubby little girl with big, dark eyes, a solemn face, and dark curly hair. Judging Wylie to be a good fifteen years younger in the photo, I asked, "How old is Tamra?"

"Nineteen. She's been gone for two days now, Ms. West, and I'm getting a little uneasy."

He looked away, avoiding eye contact, while he told me that as far as he could tell Tamra had taken a small overnight bag and driven off in her car without telling him where she was going or when she would be back. I've come to know when a client is editing his story; a lot of them do. And I'd bet that was what Wylie was doing.

"Have you reported this to the police?" I asked.

"I considered it, but the idea seemed pretty extreme."

Hiring a PI did not fall under this description, I supposed.

"And frankly," he went on, "I prefer to keep family matters private."

"Still," I said, "The police have a lot more resources than I do. If you're really worried—"

I broke off as Elena returned with the coffee, poured it, and quickly escaped.

While we stirred and sipped, he said, "Look, Ms. West, I'm not ready to put my daughter's face on milk cartons or bumper stickers. She's not missing exactly, just unaccounted for."

He was probably right. Anyway, I had no way of judging whether he was genuinely alarmed but not psychologically ready to call in the police, if he was just a control freak, or if he was a concerned parent who could afford to indulge his overprotective instincts. Whatever his motives, the case met my criteria for nonviolence, and, the economy being what it was, I had good reason to look for his daughter.

I asked him for a recent photo, and he put down his cup, went to the desk for a snapshot, and handed it to me. In it a stick-thin young woman with long straight hair stood next to a big palomino horse. The curls had vanished along with the baby fat, but if anything the eyes looked even bigger, staring out of the gaunt face.

"Tamra's horse?" I asked.

"No, it belongs to a neighbor."

"I have to ask you, Mr. Wylie—do you know if Tamra drinks or takes any kind of drugs?"

"Certainly not," he snapped.

I filed that with a large grain of salt and said, "Has she ever gone off like this before?"

"Not without checking in."

"She does visit friends?"

"Yes, of course."

"And relatives?"

"Just her mother," he said with obvious distaste. "Tamra isn't there, and she hasn't called Marilyn."

Reluctantly he told me that he and Marilyn had divorced when Tamra was three and that he had always had custody of his daughter. If there was a hidden drama there, he didn't hint at it.

School? Tamra was a bright girl, he said, but not very motivated. She was going to Saddleback Community College with plans to transfer to UC Santa Barbara. I wondered if these were her plans or his. At any rate, she had not shown up for classes.

"Boyfriend?" I asked.

"Nobody serious. There was this boy—Lee Gersky, but I'm pretty sure that's all over. I did try to call him. His roommate said he'd moved. And I called some of her friends, but nobody knew where Tamra went." He shifted in his chair. "Do you think you can find Tamra for me, Ms. West?"

I thought I could and that it was an easy way to make a few bucks. The young woman was probably off defying daddy and having a good time. If she had credit cards, it should be a simple matter to pick up a paper trail. She did, several from department stores plus Visa, American Express, and a bank debit card.

I told Wylie how much I charged and what I needed for a retainer. I thought he was going to give me an argument, but after a second he agreed, adding that of course he'd expect a strict accounting.

"Naturally." I put down my cup and picked up my briefcase. "I'll need a list of the people you contacted plus anybody else you can think of, the neighbor who owns the horse, for instance. Also credit card numbers and the license plate of her car."

He promised to fax everything to my office right away.

"And if I could keep the photo?"

"Of course."

"Just one more thing. I'd like to see Tamra's room."

"Her room? Why?" He was instantly suspicious. I had a feeling suspicion was his first reaction to anything that caught him off guard. "Is that really necessary? I don't like the idea of your going through her things."

"It's not essential," I said. "And I won't poke around. I just want an impression. Sometimes it helps. You never know."

He looked skeptical but agreed and went over to the desk to call Elena on the intercom. When she arrived, he had a few private words with her, then said, "Elena will take you up. If you have any questions afterward, let me know. Otherwise, please keep me informed."

Mr. Warmth.

With Wylie for a father I wondered if Tamra had turned to Elena for any kind of relationship. I waited until we reached the top of the stairs to ask.

"Elena, did Tamra talk about her trip to you?"

Elena shook her head.

"Did she mention planning anything with her friends? A concert up in L.A. maybe?"

"She say nothing to me, *señora.*"

Elena stopped, opened a door, and stood there, her face impassive, looking like she planned to stay. Wylie must have told her to stand guard. I went in. My first impression was that Tamra had stripped the room bare, taking all her personal belongings with her. On second glance I realized the starkness was deliberate, a retreat from the darkness and clutter of the rest of the house.

The furnishings consisted of a single bed and one of those low entertainment centers housing a television set, some sleek-looking stereo components, and bookshelf speakers. A pile of big pillows in black and white fabrics was stacked on the floor where a white rug covered most of the dark wood. A white down comforter on the bed. Bare white walls. Track lighting. The curtainless window let in as much sun as possible.

"Have you cleaned in here since Tamra left?" I asked.

After the slightest hesitation, Elena said, "She does not want me to."

What did the room say about Tamra? A healthy determination to be her own person? Or just total alienation? In any case, standing there I was sure that

Wylie was the last person to know what went on in his daughter's life.

A walk-in closet offered some normal clutter: shoes, a pile of dirty jeans, expensive cowboy boots. Lots of clothes filled the padded hangers, mostly in somber neutral tones. There might be secrets hidden in the built-in shelves and drawers but I couldn't look for them, not now.

I asked, "Do you know what she took with her?"

Elena shrugged and shook her head.

"Did you see her leave?"

Once again she hesitated. "No, *señora*."

"You were here?"

"*Sí*."

But not wearing blinders and ear plugs, although I'd bet she had to act as if she did to work in this house, and I was willing to bet that while Elena's answers were not lies, they were not complete truths.

Without a complete search Tamra's bath held no clues either. Back in the bedroom, I paused beside the window. The view was more restricted than you might imagine. Even though the Wylies lived on top of a hill, so did everybody else. Over the roof of the one-story house next door I could see *down* to a hillside pasture with a small barn and rows of overgrown oleander following the fence lines. In the picture of Tamra and the horse, there had been a building in the background. Maybe a barn. Possibly this one, although I saw no horse from my bird's-eye view.

Make that a crow's-eye view. A couple of the big birds circled lazily above the neighboring yard.

Right then I got an inexplicable urge to go downstairs, give Benjamin Wylie back his retainer, and hotfoot it out of there. Oh yeah, paying attention to my instincts would have saved me a hell of a lot of trouble, all right.

"Señora?" Elena said.

I turned away from the window and followed her downstairs, thanked her, and left, lecturing myself sternly about this tendency of late to wimp out.

Outside, the sky had turned a bright, hard blue and a sudden gust of wind whipped through the pine trees and rattled the palm fronds. Maybe the noise startled the crows. A couple of them flew up out of the yard next door to perch on a gate in the high stuccoed wall that extended out from the side of the house's garage.

The wind had also changed direction, so I caught a blast of the putrid scent I'd smelled earlier about the same time I saw the gore crusted on the bird's beaks. I picked up some lava rocks from the planter beds and hurled them, surprising both myself and the crows with my fury, drawn to the wooden gate with its black metal hinges and trim, the smell intensifying the closer I got.

So I wasn't surprised at all by what I found when I opened the gate and went into the yard.

TWO

THE WOMAN LAY just where the sidewalk joined the patio in back, her body on the cement, her head and shoulders in the star jasmine that edged the walk. Not Tamra. This woman was blond and weighed more. I'm sure there were other differences, but she had been there for a while and the crows and a big black buzzard had been doing their job, were still doing it.

I made shooing motions, and the birds flapped off. Nothing could be done about the ants and the flies. Nature's cleanup crew sometimes arrives and goes to work even before the final death rattle.

Stomach roiling, I fumbled in my purse for a small tube of petroleum jelly, one that I normally use for lip balm, and squeezed out a blob for each nostril. This helped a little, but the smell was already up inside my head and even stronger inside the yard.

I thought about going back to the van for my gun. I didn't have the Beretta yet, but my .38 was there, locked in the glove box. I dismissed the idea. Whoever had killed the woman was long gone, and if I had the weapon I doubted I could restrain myself from blasting the crows that had already returned to perch on the wall.

The birds watched as I skirted the body and entered the patio. Although I had immediately assumed murder, it was entirely possible the woman had dropped dead of natural causes. In this stage of decomposition only the coroner would know for sure, but I thought somebody had hit her hard enough so her skull was caved in just above the empty left eye socket. Tamra Wylie had split two days ago—pray God she had. Because the woman was dressed in shorts and a tank top, I could see the effects of putre-faction, and I thought she had been here at least that long. The timing could just be coincidence; still I had to look, dreading that I might find Tamra hadn't run away after all.

Nothing on the brick and concrete surfaces except a ghetto blaster beside a chaise lounge, an overturned bright blue plastic glass, a bottle of Banana Boat sun-tan lotion. Just some leaves and a fine skim of pollen in the pool. No skinny, dark-haired young woman in the lush plantings of hibiscus and gazania.

An open sliding patio door led into a family room off a large kitchen. I stood, staring in. Dread clapped a heavy arm around my shoulders, keeping me there, and I found myself straining to hear something over the quiet hiss and burble of the pool equipment and the flapping of an umbrella that shaded a square patio table.

Nothing.

I went in, taking care not to touch anything, watch-ing where I put my feet. The sound of the refrigerator was abnormally loud in the silent kitchen. A couple of bar stools stood next to an extension of a white tiled counter that served as a breakfast bar. The counter beside the sink held a bottle of Gilbey's gin and some generic tonic water, an ice cube tray with a little warm water in the bottom, a striped pink and white dish towel, a cutting board and a paring knife, and half a lime on the maple board, the edges curled and brown. The petroleum jelly wasn't doing much good because I could smell the odor of rotting citrus.

In the family room nothing looked out of place except that a brown leather purse had been dumped out on a coffee table. Amid the jumble of lipstick, Kleenex, and keys—all the typical detritus in a woman's handbag—a wallet lay open. A quick tour of the house showed no more bodies, barring the possibility that one was hidden somewhere and somehow packaged so it didn't stink.

I got out of there fast and went to call 911 on my cellular phone. The interior of the van felt like a blast furnace. The breeze had developed a searing edge that meant it was coming in off the desert and promised a full-blown Santa Ana by nightfall.

Laguna Hills is a full-fledged city now but, like the other areas rushing to incorporate, finds it cheaper to retain the services of the Orange County Sheriff's Department rather than set up its own police force.

I figured the response time would be at least five minutes, maybe ten, so I exchanged my heels for sandals and went back up to Wylie's door to ring the bell. When a surprised Elena answered, I said I needed a bathroom first and then I would speak to Mr. Wylie.

I wiped my nose and splashed cold water on my face and arms. There wasn't much I could do about the silk blouse, which already stuck to my skin, but I took off the hose, disposed of them in the wastebasket, and slipped my bare feet into the huaraches.

This must have been a slow day for crime. When I came out of the downstairs powder room, I could hear sirens, muted by distance and the thick brick walls, but coming fast. Wylie must have heard them too, and I suppose Elena had told him about my hasty return. He met me in the entry as I headed back to the front door.

"What is it?" he asked. "What's going on?"

"I'd better explain outside."

There was no time to soft-pedal the news because two patrol cars were screaming up the hill as we went out.

"I found a body," I said.

I saw the shocked dread in his eyes and added quickly, "Not Tamra. Who lives next door, Mr. Wylie?"

"The Sannermans, Robb and Kate Sannerman. You mean somebody's dead over there?"

"I'm afraid so. A woman. Blond, about five eight."

"My God—*Kate?*"

I left him standing there as the black and whites arrived, three cars from the Orange County Sheriff's Department, patrolmen piling out. I could hear more sirens wailing. As I said, a slow day and everybody looking for excitement.

There was still Vaseline in my nose. I took out a tissue and blew. No point advertising the fact that I had taken a look in the yard and house. The place would soon be officially a crime scene. Only cops were allowed to trample evidence.

I told the patrolmen what I'd found, told them who I was, and produced my ID and the state ticket which confirmed that I'm a licensed private investigator.

By now a small crowd had gathered, mostly the people who took care of the big houses, their babble a mixture of Spanish, Japanese, and Vietnamese. Very few of the inhabitants seemed to be at home, or at least they hadn't come out to gawk.

Wylie and a patrolman stood in the shade of the pine trees, the officer asking questions and taking notes, Wylie shaking his head. I didn't see Elena.

I sought refuge under a leafy jacaranda in the Sannermans' front yard and told my story to another cop, keeping it simple and only saying that I'd been visiting my client and discovered the body by chance. Of course I knew I'd have to repeat my story in a lot more detail when the investigative team arrived.

The cop decided it would be all right if I got out of the heat while I waited. Benjamin Wylie stood in front of his house apart from the crowd. I went to join him.

"It *is* Kate, isn't it?" His face was ashen and shiny with sweat. "What happened to her?"

"I don't know for sure how she died," I said, "and we'll have to wait for a positive ID, but it's probably Mrs. Sannerman. Do you know how to get in touch with her husband?"

"No. I've no idea. He travels a lot." He turned and headed for the front door, muttering something about the heat.

I followed, welcoming the chill dimness of the entry. I saw Elena as I tagged along with Wylie to his den, just a fleeting glimpse as she retreated back into the living room. Wylie either didn't see her or maybe she was just a fixture to him, unnoticed until he needed something. He went straight to a cabinet in the corner of the den, opened it to reveal a built-in bar, and took out a bottle of Glenlivet.

"Do you want some?" he asked.

I shook my head. He poured a shot glass full, downed the whiskey in a gulp, then blotted his face on a paper napkin.

"Christ, what a terrible thing," he said. "Do you have any idea what happened? Kate was a young woman."

"I think she was murdered," I said.

"Good God, right next door?"

He sounded as though the proximity of the crime bothered him more than the act itself.

"Mr. Wylie, we don't have a lot of time," I said. "We have to talk about Tamra."

"Tamra? What about her?"

"Tamra left two days ago. I'm no forensic specialist, but I'm fairly sure Mrs. Sannerman has been dead for approximately that long."

He turned to stare at me in horror. "Do you know what you're saying? You think Tamra—that she's—*involved* somehow?"

"I think it's a possibility."

"No—no, no. How could she be?"

I could think of several scenarios, most them grimmer than what I now suggested. "Maybe she saw something, got scared, and ran away."

"That's—it's absurd. If she was frightened, she would have come to me."

Even though I'd never met his daughter, somehow I doubted that. There was no getting around it. The words had to be said. I just wished I'd taken him up on the drink. "Look, Mr. Wylie, this isn't meant to scare you. God knows I hope it isn't true. If Tamra witnessed the crime, she could be in big trouble.

There's also a chance Tamra may have been a victim herself.''

"No, that's not how it happened.''

"But you can't *know* that.''

"Yes, I can. Earlier—well, I didn't tell you everything.''

Big surprise. I waited while he poured himself some more whiskey.

"I was here when she left,'' he said. "We had an argument. She ran off to her room—to sulk, I thought. Then a few minutes later she came down with her overnight bag and ran out the door. I followed her, and I saw her get into her car and drive away.''

"What did you argue about?''

"That's personal and unrelated.''

"Why not let me be the judge of that?''

"*No.* Forget it. The important thing is she didn't go next door.''

He was going to stonewall, either out of principle or some misguided mania for privacy. I hoped he didn't live to regret it.

"Okay,'' I said. "But the police may want more details.''

"The police? You haven't told the police about Tamra?''

"Not yet.''

"Well, you damn well better *not* tell them. There's a matter of confidentiality here.''

I couldn't decide which he considered more troubling: the fact that his daughter might be mixed up in a murder or that the police might think she was.

"I'll do what I can, Mr. Wylie. But if this is a homicide investigation, client privilege only goes so far.''

"If," he said. "You don't know for sure that Kate was murdered, do you?"

"No."

"Well, until you do—"

I hadn't heard the doorbell, but now we both heard voices in the hall. The patrolman who took my report earlier followed Elena in. He said the investigator from Special Assignments was ready for me. I went with him.

Wylie came along, putting a hand on my arm to stop me at the door while the patrolman walked out, saying in a fierce whisper, "Remember what I said about Tamra."

I pulled away and left him, not promising anything.

THREE

THE PATROLMAN TOOK ME in the Sannermans' front door where a narrow aisle had been marked off with slick yellow tape through the house to the patio. Outside, the crime scene had been secured, a perimeter delineated with more of the tape which enclosed most of the back yard. At least I was upwind from the corpse. I caught a whiff of cigar smoke mixed with the putrid smell. The deputy coroner puffed away on a big black stogie, an old trick to mask the odor, and only marginally more effective than my petroleum jelly.

There were a lot of people in the yard. Finding a murderer is a labor-intensive job. And in a death like this one, murder must be assumed and evidence collected, just in case. In the crowd I recognized Gary Hofer about the time the patrolman pointed him out as the investigator for the Sheriff's Special Assignments Unit.

Gary and I had been in the Police Academy at the same time and served in the LAPD, Foothill division, back in the dear dim past. I hadn't seen him in at least ten years, but I knew him all right. He was my age, mid-thirties edging toward forty. Not a big man but lean and fit, about five ten, the kind of body earned by diligent exercise, displayed with modest conceit in a tailored gray suit, a pearl gray shirt, and one of those flower-print ties that was toned down just enough to be borderline tasteful.

He stood on the patio on the other side of the open sliding door. I stepped out and waited, but he ignored me while he finished speaking to one of the field investigators. This gave me time to note that even though his light mouse-brown hair was expertly cut and blow-dried it was thinning enough so a lot of his scalp showed through, gleaming a little pink from the hot sun.

Good old Gary. We had never been buddies in the past. I doubted we would be now or in the foreseeable future. I knew Gary to be competitive, conniving, and politically astute, all of which stood him in good stead in the department. He'd told me once what he thought of ball-breaking broads, so I had no doubt of his feelings for me.

Maybe he'd mellowed, had his consciousness raised, turned into a decent human being.

Sure.

He finally turned and gave me a twitch of his lips that just barely passed for a smile. "Delilah—I wondered when I'd run into you. Seems as though I'm always reading your press coverage, how you keep finding bodies, and now you found one for me."

"Nice to see you too," I said. "How long have you been in Orange County?"

"Seven—eight months—"

The print tech cut in to ask him something. Gary took the woman aside, making a point of lowering his voice so I couldn't hear. He took out a pair of mirrored sunglasses and put them on. Not a bad idea considering the glare. I took mine out, too, and wondered what Gary was doing in Orange County.

The last I heard he was still sharpshooting his way
to the top in the LAPD. At the rate he was going he
should be heading his own division by now. I'd like to
think he was down here in the hinterlands because of
some nice juicy scandal that got him kicked out of the
department, but given the state of his wardrobe and
the way he fairly oozed assurance, I thought this was
probably not the case. When he finished with the tech,
he brushed past me and stepped inside to talk to the
team working the family room. I knew he was deliberately making me wait and not a damn thing I could
do about it.

The sun beat down on my head, and sweat ran down
my temples. The wind didn't help at all. All it did was
whip up dust from the pasture and make the job
tougher for the crime lab people. I squinted from the
glare and stared down at the hillside.

High adobe walls enclosed the yard on the sides and
the front, but there was only a chain link fence across
the back with a gate providing access to the pasture. I
could see the small barn down the hill, the one I'd seen
from Tamra's window. Still no sign of a horse, but I
assumed there had been one at some point. I wondered if it was the horse in the picture with Tamra.

A hot gust of wind swept more leaves and dust into
the pool and snapped the big blue umbrella. I went
over to join a cop who stood in the shade beside the
patio table. I knew the man, MacReedy, an old-timer
in the sheriff's department, a guy with a barrel chest
and a face like a slab of seasoned oak.

He nodded hello, then said, "Must be a hundred
degrees. Damn wind just kills my sinuses."

In Southern California the weather takes precedence in any conversation.

"I know what you mean," I said. "Listen, Mac, has anybody checked out the pasture?"

"I don't know. Why?"

I hesitated, weighing my obligation to respect Wylie's demand for confidentiality against my fears for his daughter.

"Just a thought," I said.

He considered. Nodded. "I'll give it a look."

He left me to enjoy the scant shade, which wasn't a whole lot better than standing in the sun, but at least my brief conversation with MacReedy had twigged Gary's attention. He headed back over to make sure I didn't get too comfortable or too chummy with the hired help.

"Okay," he said. His smile showed a few more teeth—capped and veneered, I'd bet. "Pretend I haven't talked to the responding patrol officer and give it to me from the top. You know the drill."

Down at the fence, I saw MacReedy and another cop go out the gate into the pasture. Over in the ground cover beyond the pool, one of the field investigators carefully extracted a hammer from the gray-green leaves and bright yellow flowers. Gary caught that, but he didn't notice MacReedy.

I repeated my story, how I had come to see Benjamin Wylie and on my way back to my van noticed the birds and then the smell.

"I had a bad feeling," I said. "So I opened the gate."

"You didn't think it might be a good idea to ring the doorbell first? That you were trespassing on private property?"

"No, I didn't."

"I remember that about you," he said. "How you play by your own rules. Okay, you go in the yard and you see the body. Did you decide to do some sleuthing? Say, check out the patio? Or maybe go into the house?"

I'm sure he was giving me his penetrating cop stare. This would have worked better if he'd taken off his sunglasses.

I looked straight through my brown oversize lenses at his gray aviators and said, "Of course not. Did you get a preliminary cause of death?"

"Official police business, Delilah. You know that. What do *you* think she died from?" he asked cagily.

"Offhand? I'd say blunt-force trauma."

"Oh? Why would you say that?"

"Gee, I don't know, Gary. Maybe because I saw Mrs. Sannerman's head, and now I see your people picking up a hammer and bagging it."

I might have mentioned robbery for a motive, but then he would know I had lied about being in the house because when the patrolman walked me through, I noticed the purse had already been picked up by Forensics.

On the hillside MacReedy had worked his way to the barn and was going inside.

Gary ignored my comment, asked, "You're sure you don't know anything about the deceased?"

"No."

"You never met her before or discussed her with anybody?"

"No."

"What are you working on for Mr. Wylie?"

"It's confidential. Unrelated to this." Well, it probably was.

Gary didn't like it, but he had a lot more important fish to fry, so he gave me a curt little nod. "Well, okay for now. But if this turns out to be homicide, we'll talk in my office, and I'll expect your full cooperation."

No chance for a comeback because he turned on his heel and left for a look at what must be the murder weapon and no ifs about it. I hung around for a moment, enduring the heat, rummaging in my purse because I was sure Gary was keeping an eye on me, waiting until MacReedy and the other cop came out of the barn. They headed back up the hill at a leisurely clip. MacReedy saw me watching and shook his head. Nothing.

I made a show of finding my keys for Gary's benefit and staged a quick exit.

At least Tamra's body was not in the house or out on the hillside. Her father was probably right. She had not been near the murder scene. She had stormed off in a snit and was holed up someplace, enjoying the fact that he was worrying about her.

Made sense.

So **why** was I having such a hard time believing it?

The crowd in the cul-de-sac had thinned a little. Most of the people who tended the big houses had gone back to work. I could hear the distant whine of a lawn mower, the louder noise of a leaf blower.

In this neighborhood there would always be gardening crews and pool men coming and going. Even if the residents of the big houses kept their windows tightly shut the way Wylie did, why hadn't one of the workers noticed the death stench coming from the Sannermans' back yard? But then, of course, maybe one of them had. Maybe even somebody who worked for the Sannermans.

If Gary Hofer hadn't already thought of this, he soon would. I disliked the man, and I remembered he was not the quickest and the brightest of cops. I also remembered he was methodical and thorough. Another thing: Barring some logical explanation for that hammer and assuming Kate Sannerman had not died of natural causes, my instincts told me this would be a high-profile case with lots of media attention. And, Lord knows, Gary's political instincts were much more finely honed than mine.

So Gary would plot all the comings and goings around here for the last few days. Easy for him; a big job for me, maybe a job Wylie wouldn't pay for because it meant he'd have to face the fact that Tamra could be involved. It certainly would be nice if I could get Gary to share that information.

Diplomacy lessons came to mind.

Charm school.

Hell.

There was nothing I could accomplish here under the nose of Orange County's finest, so I might as well head for the office. Just about the time I reached my van, a midnight blue BMW pulled into the cul-de-sac, braked suddenly and stopped in the middle of the circular street. The car was pointed at the Sannermans' driveway, which was presently occupied by two patrol cars and the Forensics van, the white vehicle labeled *Orange County Coroner*. There were more unmarked cars on the street and three uniformed officers stood around at the foot of the driveway.

The driver got out of the BMW, a lanky man with dark hair, his shirtsleeves rolled up to the elbows, his tie loosened. I had a good idea who he was. If I hurried over, I could be the one to break the news to him about his wife, maybe even get in a question or two.

I couldn't do it.

I stood there while he rushed toward the house. The cops intercepted him. I was close enough to hear him say, "I *live* there—what happened? Kate? Is it—?"

I didn't hear the cop's reply, just Robb Sannerman's anguished "Oh, *Jesus—*" as he brushed past them and plunged into the house.

FOUR

I STARTED THE ENGINE, turned on the air conditioner in the van, and sat there, isolated from the heat and the anguish in the Sannerman house while I called my office and explained to Danny why I had been delayed. Danny Thu is my part-time assistant, full-time at the moment while waiting for school to start. He goes to UC Irvine, doing a double major in business and computer science.

"Are you taking the Wylie case?" he asked.

"Yes. He'll be faxing some information. Anything urgent there?"

Midway through his recitation of phone calls and paperwork questions, I closed my eyes against the glare of the sun on the windshield and rubbed my temples, wishing I could go straight home for a long shower and a cold beer, but saying instead, "Okay, I'm on my way." In my business I've been too close to failure to take success for granted, and success means you put in a little extra time and hustle harder.

I drove over to the San Diego freeway and headed north toward the junction with the Santa Ana. The El Toro Y, as it's called, is officially designated as the second-worst freeway interchange in the county. Here traffic at the best of times resembles a computer simulation of an atomic mass on the verge of going critical: electrons and neutrons boinging around, narrowly avoiding the collisions that are sure to come. At three-thirty the rush hour had already begun. The road wasn't jammed yet, but movement was down to a sluggish crawl.

A massive widening project began a couple of years ago and construction looks to go on into the next century. At some point, we are told, this junction known as the El Toro Y will be a model of efficiency, twenty-four lanes at its widest point, with flyovers and collector roads to redirect the tangle of cars. This is all assuming, of course, that the county and the state do not go broke.

Meanwhile, beyond the Y, a portion of the project has been completed. But the freeway balloons out only to be constricted again a few miles north. There, shoulders no longer exist. Instead, narrow lanes are crammed between cement pylons topped with big plywood sheets. Just to keep things interesting, every few nights Cal Trans moves the barriers and switches the traffic flow around. I presume there is some logic to these changing detours, but since most of the work is hidden from view, sometimes I wonder if this is done just to keep us motorists on our toes.

The slow pace of the traffic gave me time to observe that taggers had been at work marking the sides of buildings in a shopping plaza with red and black graffiti. Until a couple of years ago the defacing scrawls were confined to the worst sections of L.A. and Santa Ana. Now the stuff was everywhere, especially along the freeways, but it still gave me a chill to see it here in south county. The barbarians were at the gates, leaving their message in spray paint and broad-tip markers, and nothing was safe.

For some reason this ugly intrusion of urban blight increased my sense of urgency about finding Tamra Wylie. I've looked for a lot of people and found most of them, learning in the process that there are few shortcuts, that usually the best approach is to be slow and methodical. But then *usually* I'm not beginning my search just after finding a decomposing body and feeling convinced that my missing person is connected to the murder and may even be next on the killer's list.

I decided I'd ask Danny to stay late and start on the computer work as soon as Benjamin Wylie faxed us the necessary information. Meanwhile, I'd prioritize the stuff on my desk, put off whatever I could, and clean up the rest.

By the time I got to the office the wind had died down a little. However, I knew from the desert dryness of the air and the aching blueness of the sky there would be high winds tonight, a hundred-plus temperature tomorrow and, unless we were very lucky, brush fires soon afterward.

I saw a parking spot on the street and grabbed it, came in the building the front way, and hurried up the stairs to avoid Harry Polk, the janitor, who has appointed himself my watchdog.

The building is three stories high, bland and basic, with nothing to recommend it except that it's located near the Orange County Civic Center. I have two rooms on the second floor with new carpeting, woodwork, and paint, but this is only because a letter bomb recently made redecorating a necessity. Several tenants moved out after the bombing. The offices on either side of mine are still empty. In two months, when the lease expires, I figure I'm in for either a whopping rent increase or an eviction notice.

Danny has his computer set up in the outer office where he does double duty as my receptionist. I sailed in, ready to launch into my agenda, and stopped short because Danny, my inscrutable Oriental, has a face that's an open book. I read excitement and a smidgen of conspiratorial guilt as he tilted his head toward the inner office and said, "Company."

"Who—?"

He jumped up, gathered envelopes, and reached for his backpack. "Think I'll make a mail run."

"Danny—"

He headed out the door, saying, "Back in a little while."

I have one comfortable chair in my office: mine. The other two are straight-backed and thinly cushioned. The kind of clients I get I don't want to encourage to stay for long cozy chats. Erik Lundstrom had settled in behind my desk, sideways with his long legs stretched out and crossed at the ankles. His slim leather briefcase was open at his elbow, and he was reading some kind of slick-covered prospectus.

His blue, blue eyes looked at me over the top of a pair of those half-lens reading spectacles. I'd never seen him wearing the glasses. Reminders of time moving on, those and his prematurely silver hair; not that Erik was old, but he would soon be a young, vital fifty. Still, ridiculous how the things made him look so appealingly vulnerable because I know there's not a helpless bone in that lean, hard-muscled body.

"You're here already," he said and smiled.

My heart gave a traitorous leap. I was suddenly
aware of my silk blouse stained with dried sweat and
my bare feet in the woven leather sandals. I've been
wearing my hair in a short, punky cut, but the style
had begun to remind me of my father's GI crewcut so
I was letting it grow. Earlobe length, it requires lots of
gel and spray to tame the unruly cinnamon brown
spikes. The wind had long since destroyed all the control I'd applied that morning.

Erik, of course, looked cool and immaculate in a
gray suit with a subtle blue weave, a snowy white shirt,
and a dark blue silk tie; not a hair out of place.

"I didn't mean to appropriate your desk." He put
the prospectus into his briefcase, took off the glasses,
tucked them in a pocket, and stood up. "With the
traffic these days I thought I might have a wait."

He came around one side of the desk, and I
clomped around the other and sank down.

"Yeah, it's bad all right," I said. "Too many people and too many cars."

I might have added it was Erik and all the other Orange County land developers who had gotten us into
this sorry mess. I might have except that my chair still
retained the warmth of his body, and I found myself
caught in my usual quandary of emotions, somewhere between belligerence and teenage lust.

"I really wish you'd called," I said.

"I did. Fourteen times at last count. We actually
spoke twice, I think." He pulled up one of the client
chairs and sat across from me.

"Sorry. I've been busy."

"You've been stalling. You promised me a lunch."

"I said I'd think about it."

"You've had plenty of opportunities to say no," he said softly.

And still could.

Instead I said lamely, "Well, okay, but I'm afraid it'll have to wait. I just started a new case."

"Out of town?"

"No, but—"

"You're not giving up food?"

"No—"

"Then let's decide a time and a place."

"Well . . . maybe next week."

"Saturday."

"Okay," I said ungraciously. "I guess if you want to meet me at Mom's—"

He raised a questioning eyebrow.

"Mom's Kountry Kooking," I said and gave him the cross streets. Crowded and noisy with fast service—the place would be perfect.

But he gave me a knowing grin and said, "My father warned me never to play cards with a man named Doc or eat in a place called Mom's. Let's say the Harborside in Newport Beach at one o'clock." He picked up his briefcase and left, pausing at the door to add, "See you in a couple of days."

Danny arrived about ten seconds later, his timing so perfect I was sure he was hanging around waiting for Erik's exit. He still had the envelopes in his hand.

"I thought you were going to mail those," I said.

"I was, but Harry's gone off somewhere and the storeroom's locked."

Danny leaves his bike down there. He rides to work and almost everywhere else, sometimes adding another hundred miles on the weekend just for fun. As a result his body carries no fat, and he's so full of energy he seems to be in motion even when he's sitting down.

"Mr. Lundstrom came right after you called," Danny said. "I didn't know if you wanted to see him, or if I should get rid of him or what."

He paused for me to jump in with an answer.

Like I had one.

"Don't worry about it," I said. "Did Wylie's fax come?"

He said it had and went to get it, looking disappointed. I know there's a lot of excited speculation among Danny and the rest of my friends about the rich and gorgeous Mr. Lundstrom. Most of them think I'm nuts not to snap him up. Sometimes I think so, too. But I didn't want to discuss it, and right now I especially didn't want the distraction.

According to Wylie's fax the credit cards were in his name, so checking them should be no problem. He had neglected to list the bank account information so we could find out about ATM transactions. Other factual data included the plate number of Tamra's 1992 Honda Integra. In addition, Wylie had included his ex-wife's address and phone numbers for her home and the interior design company where she worked, also addresses and phone numbers for three of Tamra's friends. For Lee Gersky there was just an address, this one with a question mark and the notation *not current*. Either the girl was a loner or her father knew damn little about her private life. Well, it was a place to start.

Danny got busy with the computer, and I began making calls. My stomach rumbled, reminding me that it was getting close to dinner. This used to be a good time to reach people. Now, everybody seems to eat out. Those who are at home don't want to be, and they certainly don't want to talk to a private investigator. Mostly I left messages on machines, including one for Tamra's mother. The one person I talked to confirmed what she'd told Wylie: she hadn't seen Tamra in the past two days and had no idea where she was. Actually, the young woman was vague on exactly *who* Tamra was and seemed annoyed rather than worried to be asked about her.

Directory assistance had no listing for Lee Gersky. I called his old number, got no answer, and left a message.

Danny ordered a pizza, and we ate it while I alternated phone calls with playing office catch-up. It was almost nine o'clock when Marilyn Wylie finally returned my call. She said she had worked late, then gone to dinner, that she was shocked to hear about Kate Sannerman's death but was not at all alarmed by Tamra's disappearance. Mainly she was disgusted that Wylie had hired me to look for her daughter.

"I just can't believe that man," she said. "A private detective, for God's sake."

"He hasn't heard from Tamra and he's worried. Frankly, after what happened next door I think he has reason."

"Well, I don't. My daughter just needed to get away for a few days. And you don't have to tell me about Ben Wylie. Tamra's getting a little independent, and it's driving him crazy. He's wasting your time and his money, Ms. West. I know Tamra's fine."

"I hope you're right," I said. "But I'd still like to make sure."

I asked for names of Tamra's other friends and acquaintances and for Gersky's number, but she either couldn't or wouldn't give me anything. I thought about shocking her with a graphic description of Mrs. Sannerman's corpse and some of my grim scenarios concerning her daughter, but I wasn't certain it would accomplish much, and she was sure to call Wylie and complain.

At some point I might have to convince Mrs. Wylie that the situation was serious, but I decided to hold off until I'd talked to everybody on Wylie's list. Meanwhile Danny might get lucky and come up with a paper trail.

I told Danny we were calling it a day.

The drive home, a shower, a double brandy. One way or another I managed to put off thinking about Erik until I was in bed—and *that* little irony didn't escape me at all.

Probably I should just sleep with the guy and get it out of my system. But I don't have casual affairs, and while I might not have to be madly in love with a man to have sex with him, at least I have to *like* him. And I wasn't sure how I felt about Erik.

When I first met him the attraction had been mutual and instantaneous, and he'd deliberately used my feelings and the offer of a job on his security staff to distract me from a case I was working on. Afterward, to make amends, he made sure my name got around to all his wealthy, influential Orange County friends. My business boomed, which was all very nice—until I began to feel as though every facet of my life was being quietly stage-managed.

The words manipulative and controlling come to mind. Also concerned and caring because this is the same man who sat up nights in the hospital and paid my medical bills after the bombing, the one that destroyed my office.

So I'd give him lunch.

Maybe.

Then again, I could still change my mind.

FIVE

THE SANTA ANA WINDS arrived just after midnight, right on cue, dusty and desert-dry, rattling the windows and lashing the treetops. I had just fallen into an edgy sleep, some instinct keeping me on the alert, the old reptile brain hunkered down and prepared for the worst. In the common area of my apartment complex, something went clanging along the pavement and hit a dumpster with a resounding thump, startling me awake. When I finally went back to sleep, the crows kept flapping into my dreams, a whole squadron of them, cutting off my retreat and maneuvering me toward the gate to the Sannermans' back yard.

I had set the alarm for six, not my favorite time of the day, but this morning I was damn happy to hear the annoying little beep. I pulled on shorts and a T-shirt, laced up my sneakers, and went outside. The wind had died down, leaving the sky a harsh, scoured blue and the air so dry it instantly dried out the mucous membranes in my nose.

Never mind.

I trudged off along sidewalks littered with pine needles and palm fronds, building up to a speed walk, determined to put in my three miles.

Recently, all the health maxims have been turned upside down. Now carbohydrates are good and fat's bad. Running may keep your heart healthy but reports warn that all that pavement pounding wrecks the

knees and spine. I won't be surprised to read some-
day soon that actually we should all be eating hot
fudge sundaes and lying down when we feel the urge
to exercise.

Hedging my bets, I've given up jogging.

After a shower, I settled on a yellow cotton skirt, a
white tank top, and sandals. Not exactly proper business attire, but during a Santa Ana close enough. It
was still early so I headed over to Mom's for breakfast. The restaurant keeps a stack of papers up front
for the customers, but I was too busy saying hello to
everybody to read them right away. Mom's Kountry
Kooking doesn't have a shred of ambience. It does
have bright lighting, clean floors, and comfortable
chairs and booths. The portions are huge, good-
quality food prepared in an immaculate kitchen. Erik
didn't know what he was missing.

As far as I can tell, nobody's mother was ever involved in the business. Bernie Godchalk owns the
place, a tough, middle-aged fellow who only comes in
once a week to scrutinize the accounts. Bernie's talent
is finding qualified people and then having the good
sense to leave them alone. A while back when I'd
fallen on hard times, I used to moonlight at Mom's,
and I still play poker with some of the kitchen help.

This morning Jorge Sanchez, the cook, made me
chorizo and eggs, home fries, and a mound of sour-
dough toast. Giving up jogging is one thing, but you
have to draw the line somewhere.

When I finally got to the papers, an article officially confirmed that Kate Sannerman had been murdered. Details were sketchy. The victim died from a
blow with a blunt object; robbery had not been ruled

out as a motive. Nothing about the hammer found in the ground cover beside Kate's pool.

Had the murderer brought the weapon with him, or had it been in the house or garage? The police like to hold back facts like that. Fine with me. I certainly wasn't going to spread the word around. Come to think of it, my name wasn't mentioned in the article, and the press hadn't called. Gary Hofer was making sure I didn't get any free publicity.

As for the robbery angle, I supposed it was possible that somebody had slipped into the Sannermans' back yard, surprising Kate; that he killed her and then took whatever money he could find. But the killing blow was struck on Kate's skull above the left eye, and I remembered something my father once said. A cop for twenty years, he told me that strangers sneak up from the back; family and friends do their killing face to face.

Following that line of thought, Kate's husband would be at the top of the list of suspects, regardless of how distraught he had appeared yesterday.

My appetite vanished. Maybe I'd get lucky and find Tamra quickly, rule out any connection between Tamra and the murder, and let Gary get on with solving the crime and making a name for himself. I pushed away the rest of my breakfast, finished my coffee, and went to say goodbye to Jorge.

"The game's still on for Saturday, right?" I said.

"Sure, unless you have other plans."

"What plans?"

"I don't know. There are many things you could be doing."

Jorge and his wife, Consuelo, have become as good friends as I have in the world. They are also part of the group decision that I should have more of a social life than coming over for chili colorado and playing basketball with their kids after dinner.

"You mean like a date?" I asked.

His dark eyes flashed with excitement. "You have one?"

I was meeting Erik for lunch—always assuming I went—which would be over long before the game. Anyway our meal would not qualify as a date.

"*No.* I'm playing poker," I said firmly. "Have to give you guys a chance to get even."

At the office I was early enough to find a parking place out back. There was no chance to avoid Harry Polk. He was theoretically working on the glass door with a bottle of window cleaner and a wad of paper towels, but really was laying for me.

Harry's short and wispy with a shrunken chest and rounded shoulders under a thrift store white shirt. His tan polyester trousers were a size too big, belted over his little potbelly, the pant legs rolled up two turns. He had sprung for a haircut from a real barber, however, his thin gray hair neatly shorn for a change.

"Miz West, I didn't get to see you last night. Guess you musta worked real late."

"That's right," I said. "I have a new case."

"And I wasn't here when you got back yesterday either," he said, and I thought *uh-oh* because normally Harry bugs me for every detail about my work.

"Well, you know when your friend came to see you there wasn't any parking at all out back," he went on. "That nice Eyetalian car of his. There was no telling where he was gonna have to put it. I told him I'd better ride with him and stay with his car while he visited. And good thing, too, because the closest thing was the lot at the courthouse. That's a real beautiful automobile. I told Mr. Lundstrom I'd be happy to watch it for him any time."

"I'm sure he appreciated it," I said shortly, leaving Harry standing there at the bottom of the stairs. I'll admit I was feeling just a little miffed at being supplanted in the old man's interests by Erik's Lamborghini.

In my office, the message light on my machine blinked steadily. Three hangups and an ex-client, totally smashed and weepy, saying he was all alone in the world now and it was all my fault—never mind that he'd insisted on pictures of his wife and her lover's weekly rendezvous aboard my client's boat down in Dana Point Harbor, which gave him more than enough reason to file for divorce.

According to the time code these messages were left the night before, all prior to one A.M.; the final one had come in this morning about five minutes before I arrived: *Hi, it's Rita. Did you forget my number or what? Damn I hate these machines.*

Until recently Rita Braddock ran an answering service with real live people to take my calls. One by one her other customers had canceled the service, citing the sagging economy. I'd offered to forgo my discount, but it didn't help. Rita closed shop. Fortunately for her, she has another thriving business, a health spa she owns with her boyfriend, Farley Truitt. No matter that the shine has dulled considerably on the

Golden State, Californians are still determined to look totally buff while they stand in the unemployment line.

I really didn't want to talk to Rita. My friends come from quite different compartments of my life, but lately I've come to suspect that they are networking. Besides that, Rita has years of experience at reading every nuance of my voice and the skill of a Gestapo interrogator. She's also an expert at running me to earth, so I figured I might as well get it over with.

I dialed Ultimate Fitness and found Rita answering the phone.

"Hey, stranger," she said. "What's new?"

"What does that mean?" I replied, instantly defensive.

"Just wondering what's going on in your life."

"Jesus," I said. "Did the man send out fliers? Did he hire a skywriter? It's *lunch* for God's sake, and I don't even know if I'm going."

"If you're this mad, it can only mean your date is Erik. I guess Farley owes me ten bucks."

"You're making *bets* now?" My voice rose along with my adrenaline. "And you bet on *Erik?*"

"Well, you have to admit the man's persistent. And you may be stubborn, kiddo, but you're no fool. Uh-oh, looks like somebody's jumped their turn on the stair stepper. Gotta run before they spill blood. Call me, you hear? Full report."

On second thought I might learn to love my answering machine.

RATHER THAN WAIT for Danny and have to field more personal questions, I had left him a memo about the day's work and headed for the sheriff's department to sign a formal statement, timing my visit nicely because Gary was not around. Then, since phone calls were getting me nowhere, I went off to track down Tamra's friends.

Now, three hours later, Benjamin Wylie's short list had been supplemented by a few more names I'd picked up as I went along. Still, most of these people were high school acquaintances who had since lost touch. A couple of the others knew her from college, mostly to share notes and hang out with in the cafeteria. I was beginning to think either Tamra led a very lonely life or else a very secretive one.

One young woman named Amber did remember Tamra's boyfriend, who often waited for Tamra in the quad. Lee was too cool, Amber said with a touch of envy. They were a definite couple; oh, no, no way had they broken up. Come to think of it she'd seen the two of them together recently at a movie theater.

"Trust me," she said. "The way they were making out, they were like *nooo* problem."

Wylie's opinion about his daughter's love life was about as accurate as his knowledge of her social group.

I had wound up talking to Amber at her job in the Mission Mall, one of those trendy places designed for teenagers who had a bigger clothing allowance than I did. As it happened, the address Wylie supplied for Lee Gersky was near the mall, although Wylie had noted the information was not current. Having had no luck in reaching the ex-roommate by phone, I decided to try and find him at home.

Gersky's last known place of residence turned out to be right across the street in a complex called Hilltop Apartments. I assumed the name was a joke.

There *had* been a hill here at one time—until the builder leveled it to fill a deep ravine and create one more featureless building space.

The complex was standard Southern California issue: tile roofs and stuccoed walls painted that peculiar shade of bubble gum pink that local builders must buy in million-gallon lots. The landscaping amounted to some Indian hawthorn and jasmine with an occasional hibiscus, all stuff that was easy to grow, given enough water—and never mind those six-year droughts.

Apartments were arranged in blocks of eight, four up and four down, each pair of upper units served by a narrow landing and a stairway, dinky little patios for the people downstairs. Everybody shared a great view of the parking lot where space was at a premium, most of it marked Tenants Only, lots of trucks, jeeps, and four-by-fours mixed in with the Geos and Hyundais. I was lucky to find a slot.

Out of the van, I could hear heavy metal music blasting from an upstairs unit where the door was wide open; two guys stood outside, leaning on the wrought iron railing. I spotted my destination: 19C, right across the landing from the two men.

They were both twentysomething, dressed in shorts and tank tops designed to show off muscular shoulders and chest hair, not the best selection of wardrobe for these two, who probably spent more time drinking beer than pumping iron. Right now they were working on a couple of Coronas. It was only 11:45, but a line of dead soldiers on the edge of the landing indicated these were not the first of the day.

The two watched as I walked up the steps, their gaze stripping off my clothes. One said something, the comment drowned out by the music, and the other snickered.

I felt a hot crawl of embarrassment, following by a rush of irritation for letting these jerks bother me. Ignoring them, I went over to knock at 19C. Not much shade from the noonday sun, but the heat was moderated by cool air pouring out of their apartment, where the air conditioner must be running full blast.

A young man opened the door of 19C—maybe twenty-five, slender with curly red hair and pale skin. He wore khaki slacks and a long-sleeved shirt with a button-down collar, a light beige with a dark green stripe. Behind him the room was dim and shadowy, the blinds tightly closed and no lights switched on.

"Hi," I said, forced to raise my voice over the clamor of drums and guitars. "I'm looking for Lee Gersky. I understand he used to live here."

"Is there a problem?" he asked warily.

"Maybe. Could we talk for a minute? Sorry, I don't know your name."

"Kevin Ross."

"Kevin." I handed him my card. "Delilah West. I called last night and left a message, but I wasn't sure I had the right number."

He darted a wary glance at our audience before he looked at my card. "Oh yeah. I got your call. I just didn't have anything to tell you. Lee moved out four months ago, and I don't know where he is. Listen, I gotta go. I'm late for class."

He reached down just inside the door and picked up a portfolio made of tough black nylon fabric, the zipper open and the sides bulging with books and papers, came outside, and closed the door. More unintelligible comments from the guys on the balcony behind us and mocking laughter. A dull flush reddened Kevin's ears as he jabbed the key into the lock and turned the dead bolt.

"How about after class?" I asked. "Maybe you can give me something—the name of a relative of Lee's or some friends."

"Oh, I can do that all right." He tilted his head toward his neighbors. "His best buddies are right over there. Talk to them."

He brushed past me and ran down the stairs to hoots and catcalls.

"Oooo, Kevie—"

"'Smatter, dude? The babe too much for you?"

The babe traded her disgust for what I hoped was a neutral expression and turned to face them just as a third man ambled out, this one bigger, muscle-bound and mean-eyed, and definitely dirtier. He wore cut-off jeans that hadn't seen a washing machine in recent memory and a stained black Metallica T-shirt with the sleeves ripped out. I couldn't tell what the stains were on the shirt and didn't want to know. Bristle-cut blond hair topped a broad Neanderthal forehead.

"Hey, babe, whatever you're selling we are definitely buying." This was from the fellow closest to me whose near-naked torso was covered with bronze fur a shade lighter than his bushy hair.

His friend—shorter, darker, Hispanic, stringy muscles in arms that looked too long for his body, a mustache—gave him an approving nudge in the ribs.

Something told me these boys would not be inclined to talk to either regular cops or private ones. I was pretty sure they hadn't overheard my conversation with Kevin, so I kept my business cards in my purse, smiled to show my appreciation of the wit, and said, "Hey, guys, Kevin said maybe you can help me find Lee Gersky."

"Jeez"—a hand to the furred chest in a you-stabbed-me-in-the-heart gesture. "Why would you want Lee when we're here?"

I managed a little laugh. "Oh, old friends—you know."

"Maybe you need some new friends, babe. I'm Randy. That's Carlos, and that's big bad Bix." He paused and gave me a questioning look.

"Delilah," I said.

"Dee-li-lah."

He rolled my name around like he enjoyed the taste of it, making me question once again the wisdom of parents when it comes time to name a child.

Then he said, "Come on in, and let's get acquainted."

I knew there was at least one other person in the apartment because I could see a pair of feet, large with hairy ankles, propped up on the arm of a sofa. Discretion as well as caution sure as hell was the better part of valor in this situation, but Randy caught my hesitation and there was this smirky little grin on his face, daring me to chicken out, so naturally I marched inside.

The old sofa and a coffee table were the only furniture in the room except for an entertainment center on the far wall which was loaded with high-end gadgets and a projection TV. On the forty-eight-inch screen Kermit and Miss Piggy were singing a duet, the sound muted so that what you heard was Guns n' Roses. Randy detoured to turn the stereo down a notch or two.

I counted noses and found there were three guys inside, bringing the total to six. One sprawled on a futon, sound asleep. Another was in the kitchen area, leaning on the open refrigerator door, staring intently at the contents, as though he was having a hard time deciding what to choose. The only thing in the refrigerator was beer, but hey, there were at least two different brands in there.

The third guy, the one attached to the feet, lay on his back on the sofa. He wore a pair of swimming trunks and was eating peanuts from a plastic bowl balanced on his stomach and watching the Muppets with a rapt expression. Above him a huge, skinny, gray tiger-striped cat stretched out along the back of the sofa. The place smelled of peanut oil, marijuana, and old pizza. Somewhere in the apartment I'd bet there was also a litter box.

Randy grabbed the couch potato's arm and yanked him up. A few peanuts went flying, but the guy retained most of them in his bowl, made a few feeble protests, which Randy ignored, and went to sit on the floor in front of the TV and resume eating. The cat didn't move a whisker.

"Hey, Jam," Randy yelled in the direction of the kitchen. "Coupla brews out here."

Carlos sat down on one end of the sofa. Bix hulked over to slouch on the arm next to him. Randy dropped into the other end spot, grinned at me, and patted the empty cushion in the middle.

"Uh, thanks, no. Allergies," I said, staying right where I was, two feet from the open door.

Randy grinned some more, watching me, and reached up to stroke the cat. For all his joking around there had never been a spark of humor in his cold, piggy eyes.

I thought about my .38 out in the van and then about the Beretta, ready to be picked up tomorrow and how I ought to be there waiting when the gun shop opened.

"When do you think Lee will be back?" I asked.

"Who's Lee?" Jam handed me a cold can of Budweiser Light.

"Use to live here," Carlos said.

As in the past tense.

The noisy music made my eardrums hurt, and I was getting pretty sick of the lot of them. These boys did not wear well.

"Where's Lee now?" I asked. "I'm only in town for a few days. I'd really like to get in touch with him."

The phone rang out on the kitchen counter, barely audible over the music. Bix shoved off and went to answer it.

"Lee moved around a lot," Randy said, distracted now, his attention on Bix. "If you want to leave me your number—"

"Randy." Bix put a paw over the mouthpiece and waited.

"Yeah. Listen," Randy said to me, no longer interested in whatever game he thought he was playing. "Catch you later."

He jerked his head toward Carlos who jumped up and hustled me out. He shut the door in my face and left me standing there, still holding the beer.

Clearly, I was not living up to my biblical name-sake.

I added the Bud to the line of empties on the landing, more than happy to get the hell out of there and look for Lee Gersky someplace else.

SIX

A LONE YOUNG WOMAN fielded calls in the Hilltop Apartments management office. The sign on her desk identified her as Wendy Cole. I figured at least two other people worked there, one at the desk next to Wendy's and another in the glassed-in manager's office. Wendy said everybody had gone to lunch.

Sounded like a good idea, so I went back over to the mall and found a soup and salad place. After my huge breakfast, I passed up the three-meat gumbo for a big bowl of greenery sprinkled with some low-cal Italian, a French roll, and some iced tea.

Thus fortified I went back out to my van, started up the engine, turned on the air conditioner, and called Danny. Wylie still hadn't faxed the information about Tamra's ATM card, but Danny had the credit card search in place. Judging from the company Lee Gersky kept, I decided a background check was in order—not just on Gersky but on his old roommates in 19D as well. However, I would need a bit more information about them, last names for instance.

Danny promised he'd get started right away, gave me an update on some other ongoing investigations, then said, "How does it look for Saturday?"

"What about Saturday?" I asked, immediately suspicious.

"Some of us are planning to bike down to San Diego, but if you need me—"

"No, no," I said. "You go ahead."

Driving back to Hilltop Apartments, I told myself I really was being ridiculous. Jumping to conclusions was becoming my standard reaction these days. Anyway, so what if my friends worried about me? They just wanted me to go out, have some fun, be happy. And what did I want? Oh yeah, that was the question, all right. Wasn't it lucky I had a perfect excuse to put off finding an answer?

At the management office, Wendy Cole was still on the telephone, looking more harried than ever. The sun had dropped down enough to angle in through the front windows, and even though the air conditioning was running, the room was uncomfortably warm.

At the other desk a woman—Maria Lucci according to her nameplate—pitched the complex's great location to two young men while gathering up her purse and a large key ring and escorting them out the door. Wendy gestured toward the manager's office—yes, he was in. I could see him, also on the phone. When I took a step back that way, Wendy held up a hand, definitely signaling stop.

The front area was small and crowded with the two desks, five chairs, and a display stand holding brochures. I thumbed through one while I waited. The smallest unit, one-bedroom, 650 square feet, went for $750 a month. There was a lot of wealth in Orange County, but not much of it filtered down to the kids who lived in places like Hilltop Apartments. Most worked for little more than minimum wage and had to share their living quarters with other people to make ends meet.

Sometimes the places turned into crash pads—like the one occupied by Kevin Ross's neighbors. Snatches of Wendy's phone conversations told of more headaches associated with running a complex like this: backed-up plumbing, parking violations, bounced checks. It would have been nice if I'd had a chance to ask her some questions, but no such luck. I kept my eye on the manager, and as soon as I saw him hang up the phone, I headed for his office, cheerfully ignoring Wendy's gestures for me to wait.

I gave a rap of warning, then went inside. No name on the door, just one of those plastic nameplates on his desk reading *Jerry Reeser*. He looked even more stressed out than Wendy. He wore his longish brown hair combed back from a narrow face where little wrinkles radiated from the corners of hazel eyes. What might have once been dimples were turning into straight lines carved deep in the flesh. I judged him to be about forty and showing every year. His office was slightly cooler than the reception area, but not much. A tan jacket was draped over the back of his chair, and he'd rolled up his shirtsleeves.

"Mr. Reeser? I know you're probably swamped, but could I have a word with you?" I told him who I was and handed him a card. "I'm trying to locate somebody who used to live here."

He tensed up some more, drawing his head in closer to his shoulders. If I was bringing trouble, he didn't need any, thanks. He said, "Well, sure, I guess I have a minute—" His phone rang. He pushed an intercom button, said, "Wendy, will you get that? Tell them I'll call them back." Then, to me, "Who is it you're looking for?"

"Lee Gersky."

"Gersky—" I was sure the name was familiar, but Reeser paused, shook his head. "Sorry, I don't think I—"

"He lived in 19C with Kevin Ross. Then he moved into 19D for a while."

"Oh, right. Tell you what—let me pull the file. We have over three hundred people—" He went over to extract a folder from a bank of cabinets. The phone began to ring again. He came back to stab the intercom and say tersely, "Wendy, please, give me some time here, will you?" while the insistent ringing went on. When it finally stopped, he sat down, flipped through the folder, and tugged at his tie. A muscle worked in his cheek, and a trickle of sweat ran down in front of his right ear.

"No, no forwarding address," he said. "Why are you looking for him?"

"It's connected to a case I'm working on. What about references? Maybe he listed a relative or friend on his application."

"We're not supposed to give out that information. Sorry." But he hesitated, asked, "Can you tell me what it's about?"

"Lee's girlfriend disappeared," I said. "It's vital that I talk to him."

"Oh . . . you think something happened to her?"

"I'd say it's possible." I put some grimness in my voice, easy to do with the memory of Kate Sannerman's body fresh in my mind.

He hunched his shoulders, considering, and, I hoped, wrestling with his conscience.

"Look, I'd really like to help," he said, "but the thing is Kevin Ross is the responsible party on the lease. There's nothing on Gersky. You spoke to Ross?"

I nodded. "Briefly. I got the idea they didn't part on the best of terms. He sent me over to 19D."

"And what did they tell you?"

"Not much. Not a nice bunch of guys."

"Yeah—well, they're not unique, believe me. About Gersky—tell you what, let me ask around. Maybe I can find out something."

"I'd appreciate it," I said. "Meanwhile, there's something you could do for me. Give me the last names of the fellows in 19D."

"Well," he said reluctantly, "I don't know. Why do you need that information?"

"Oh, just to fill in some holes in my report. If it's a problem, I'll ask Kevin Ross."

"No, I guess it's okay." He got up to pull the file, glanced at it briefly, and said, "Randy Beaumont and Carlos Diego."

"That's all?"

"Everybody on the lease."

The phone rang again, the sound particularly strident and shrill. Rage flared briefly in Reeser's eyes. He balled one hand into a fist and covered the distance back to his desk in two long strides. I was sure he wanted to smash the damn thing. Come to think of it, not a bad idea.

Instead, he gave me a tic of a smile, said, "I'd better get that," picked it up, sat down, and told me "I'll call you" before he said hello.

I still wanted to talk to Wendy and the other woman, but Ms. Lucci hadn't returned and a couple of prospective tenants were parked at Wendy's desk.

Later, then.

Back out in the boiling sun, I was beginning to regret leaving that beer undrunk at Randy's place. I went in search of a McDonald's where I had an icy Coke in a cool corner and tried to figure out where to go from here.

People like to think investigations are a nice orderly process, straight lines from A to B to C that form logical patterns. Hell, I'd like to think so too, but experience has taught me otherwise. In practice what I do is more like looking for a banana cream pie in a pitch-black room. If you fumble your way around long enough, eventually you'll trip and fall into the damn thing facefirst.

Obviously I wasn't going to give up on finding Lee Gersky. If Tamra was alive and well, surely she would have called her boyfriend if for no other reason than to bitch about her dad. An even more likely possibility was that she was with Lee—which put locating him at the top of my list.

Maybe I'd get lucky and Danny would find an address or Jerry Reeser might come up with something. Otherwise I'd talk to Kevin again, and, not a pleasant prospect, to Randy and his pals.

What else?

I sipped some Coke and—all right, I confess—I polished off a large order of french fries while I thought about Tamra's mother. She seemed awfully sure that her daughter was okay. Wylie had given me the impression that Tamra wasn't close to Marilyn, but this could prove to be as far off the mark as the rest of his observations.

Marilyn would be at work now. I'd catch her at home later. In the meantime I was only fifteen minutes away from Benjamin Wylie's house in Nellie Gail. I thought it couldn't hurt to go by and give him an update, maybe pry loose some of those things he wasn't telling me. I had no idea what his routine was, but if he'd gone into the office rather than working at home, well, I'd still have a chance to talk to the maid, Elena.

Driving into the development I saw few crows and no circling buzzards. Only a dark stain remained of the roadkill from the day before. I expected to find reporters camped in the cul-de-sac outside the Sannerman house, but, I suppose, like the birds the media were off looking for carrion someplace else.

The midnight blue BMW sat on the Sannermans' driveway—the husband's car. I parked the van, got out, and stood there, considering Tamra's parents were convinced that Kate's murder had nothing to do with Tamra's disappearance. I wished I was. Remembering my first sight of Kate's body and the smell of putrefaction mixed with the sweet scent of star jasmine, I went up the Sannermans' driveway and rang the bell.

I could hear somebody make several attempts before the dead bolt was turned, then the door was thrown open. Robb Sannerman leaned out, one hand on the knob, one on the doorjamb as if to bar the way, his face flushed with anger. His dark hair was uncombed, long enough to touch his collar. A lock hung down in his eyes.

"Can't you people just leave me the hell alone? I told you I'm not going to talk to you and I meant it."

I could tell a media response when I heard it.

"I'm not a reporter, Mr. Sannerman. I'm Delilah West. I found your wife yesterday."

"Oh. You're the one." His lanky frame sagged as though the anger had been propping him up.

"Yes. I'm sorry to intrude, but I'd like to talk to you. Can I come in?"

He nodded reluctantly and opened the door a little wider, then led me into the family room. Except for the fact that Kate's purse and its spilled contents were gone from the coffee table, the room looked the same as it had the day before and yet, somehow, profoundly different. Yesterday there had been only the feel of death here; now the living had moved back in.

Robb's suit coat lay in a crumpled heap on the carpet next to the sofa. His tie was draped on a chair. Out in the kitchen several days' worth of mail and newspapers had been dumped on the white tiled breakfast bar. There was also an opened bottle of Jim Beam and a glass full of amber liquid on the counter. Outside, leaves and pine needles blown in by the wind covered the water in the pool. In this heat the glass doors were closed, but I could hear the faint choked sound of a pump with a clogged skimmer.

"I couldn't stop thinking last night that if you hadn't found her, I would've come home and— God—" He went into the kitchen to pick up the glass and slug down half the contents. "Just the thought of her lying out there—sorry, do you want something? This is bourbon. I never drink bourbon, but—can I fix you one, Ms. West?"

"No, thanks. And it's Delilah."

"Delilah. I know it's early, but I'm planning on getting drunk. Maybe I'll sleep. Didn't work last night, though." Robb plowed a hand through his hair. "You sure you don't want anything? It's so damned hot out. Some pop? Water?"

He opened the freezer compartment of the double-doored refrigerator and removed a tray even though there was a dispenser for cubes or crushed ice. "The ice maker doesn't work. These damn things—" He looked down at the blue plastic tray, as though he was trying to remember what to do with it.

"That's all right, really." I came and took the tray from him, slid it back in the freezer. "Let's go sit down."

"Kate always liked crushed ice. It never mattered to me. You ever notice how all the gadgets break at the same time everything else goes to hell?"

He brought his drink and allowed me to steer him over to the sofa. He said, "I had to look at her." Robb Sannerman had basset hound eyes: huge, soft, moist, full of a blind, animal pain. "The police wanted to make sure it was really Kate."

He put the drink down and slumped over, elbows on his knees, his head in his hands, pressing the heels of his palms hard against his forehead as though he was trying to squeeze the memory from his mind.

"Sons-a-bitches," he said. "They watched me— with this—this *look* on their faces. And kept asking questions. Today, too. I told them I was out of town, but they just kept on and on, like they think *I* could have done that to Kate—*Jesus*..." He picked up his drink and gulped two big swallows.

I felt sorry for him, but I wasn't surprised. Naturally he would be a suspect. I also knew his despair didn't mean he hadn't bludgeoned his wife with that hammer. *Family and friends do their killing face to face.* Murderers may suffer terrible remorse; they may truly grieve. These emotions don't guarantee innocence. Still, I wasn't ready to judge him guilty either.

"The questioning's routine," I told him. "Did you have a lawyer with you?"

"No. I didn't think I needed one." He drained his glass. "I had to call Kate's sister up in Palo Alto to talk about the funeral. Rose is eight months pregnant, and she's having problems. She can't come down here. Anyway, the police won't say when—I mean Kate's body—it's still in the morgue. Do you know— How long will they keep her there?"

"It varies. A while. Listen, have you had anything to eat today?"

"I think I had a sandwich—part of one."

"Let me fix you something. Scrambled eggs or—"

"No, not hungry. You can make me another one of these." He held up his glass with a lopsided grin. "I think the stuff's beginning to work, at least from the knees down. Maybe one more—"

I didn't argue. I took his glass out to the kitchen and filled it, remembering suddenly those first nights after my husband Jack died, how much I just wanted oblivion and how hard it was to obtain. When I brought the drink back, Robb eyed me, the puppy-dog look turned grave and owlish.

"Why are you so kind to me? Never mind. I can use a little kindness right now. But you didn't say why you were here yesterday. Somebody said you were working for Ben—doing what?"

"I'm looking for Tamra. She left a couple of days ago, and her father hasn't heard from her since."

If I added my suspicions about Tamra's disappearance being linked to Kate's murder, it was likely he would pass the information along to the police. At that point, my client might hand me my head, and if he didn't, Gary would. Of course, there was nothing I could do if Robb reached his own conclusions. Maybe the connection wasn't all that obvious, or maybe he'd had too much booze. Anyway, he just asked, "Tamra ran away?"

"That's what her father thinks. Does that surprise you?"

"A little—I don't know."

"Do you see much of her?"

"Not really. She used to come over and ride Goldy."

So there had been a horse in the barn down the hill, the same one, I'd bet, in the picture with Tamra.

"Where's Goldy now?" I asked.

"Kate sold her."

"Did Tamra come around after that?"

"Sometimes."

He stared down into the whiskey, his thoughts turned inward. Either the booze was kicking in or he was simply tuning out. I said quickly, "Did you ever meet any of Tamra's friends? How about Lee Gersky?"

"Yeah, I met him."

Impossible to miss the bitterness in Robb's voice. He drained the rest of his drink and carefully set the glass on the coffee table.

"I take it you don't like Lee," I said.

"Between you and me—" he leaned back and closed his eyes "—I hate the little . . . bastard . . ."

Almost immediately his face went slack, and he began to take long, rhythmic breaths. Great. I didn't begrudge him the rest, God knows, but one thing was for sure. I wasn't going to find out why he hated Lee Gersky—not tonight.

SEVEN

ALTHOUGH IT WAS WONDERFUL for Robb that he could escape into sleep, it certainly would have been nice if he'd waited a few more minutes. I sighed, nudged him down so his head was on a pillow, took off his shoes, and lifted his long, limp legs up on the sofa. Lying there, he looked so totally vulnerable. Men do.

Charlie Manson probably does.

Well, no, not Charlie.

Still, I had no solid reason for thinking that Robb might have killed his wife except for suspicion born of experience. If he was innocent, I hoped the cops found themselves another prime suspect soon. I knew Gary Hofer to be relentless, and he would pick apart the seams of Robb Sannerman's life. Some people never recover from that kind of destruction.

I took Robb's empty glass out to the kitchen. The window over the sink offered a view across the back yard and down through the weedy pasture toward the empty barn. Maybe there was a pattern forming here if I could see it. Let's say Tamra hangs around the Sannerman house because of Kate's horse. Maybe Lee comes along with her. Hmmm. Any number of scenarios there. For instance: Robb hungers for sweet young flesh; Kate, observing, turns into a jealous shrew. Arguments between Kate and Robb definitely could turn explosive.

Remembering her picture, I saw near-anorexic Tamra as a sad-eyed waif rather than Lolita, so, considering Robb's reaction to Gersky's name, it could have been Kate doing the lusting after Tamra's boyfriend. From what I'd heard about Lee he wasn't my type, but there's no accounting for tastes.

This last possibility gave Robb an even stronger motive for killing his wife. Of course, it didn't let Tamra off the hook either and provided a damn good reason for her to leave town. Not to mention what Gersky's reaction might have been if Kate suddenly turned him off.

While I stood there speculating, I flipped through the stack of mail on the counter. I can't help it; I have this basic urge to snoop. It's instinctive with me, like breathing and eating.

In addition to the usual bulk-rate advertising and the Penny Saver stuffed with fliers, the pile contained mostly bills, at least a half dozen from credit card companies. There were two anonymous-looking envelopes that I recognized as being from collection agencies, having had a few from these same folks myself. One letter was from the IRS.

Having not quite satisfied the urge to pry, I moved on to the drawers and cabinets. Cheap stainless and supermarket china. A minimum of appliances and cookware. Damn little in the pantry. Less in the refrigerator.

Robb was still snoring away, so—what the hell—I headed for the living room, well aware that Gary Hofer and his crew would have given the house a thorough once-over. I'd had other concerns the day before when I made my quick tour. My impression had been that the place was sparsely furnished. Now I saw that it was downright bare, and I had the feeling this was not just a case of minimalist chic. Could be after buying the house, the Sannermans had no money left for furniture.

In the master bedroom one chest was split between the two of them. A collection of pictures sat on top. Happier times: Robb and Kate on their wedding day; Kate with a beautiful palomino horse, the same one in the picture with Tamra.

Given a makeup artist, optimum lighting, and a skilled cameraman, Kate Sannerman might have been Hollywood beautiful. She had that careless, California-blond look: pretty, self-assured, and slightly bored. I wished I could read more from the picture, something that might give me a clue about why somebody had smashed in her skull and left her for the crows and the ants.

Nothing.

Also nothing in the four-drawer chest except underwear, socks, and a jumble of costume jewelry in a small plastic bin. Kate stashed her cosmetics in the bathroom, which was in need of a good cleaning.

I found a jewelry box in the walk-in closet that adjoined the bathroom. Empty. Robb had a modest wardrobe. Kate's side was stuffed with clothes, more in the closet of a guest room down the hall. Some of the things were expensive, but at least one season old, maybe two.

The shelves in the closet held a stack of albums and boxes of the personal effects we all drag along with us through life, each labeled with a broad black marker:

Robb—Maine Township & Mich. State; Kate—CSSB; Tax Returns; Xmas Stuff.

I would have liked to sneak a peek at some of these things, but this was a reconnoiter, not a full-scale sortie.

A third bedroom was set up as an office. There was a framed certificate on the wall, announcing that Kate Sannerman was a member of the million-dollar sales club for Coast Real Estate. A desk held a computer and a box of diskettes. Too bad Danny wasn't along.

The lower right-hand drawer was about half filled with papers, no order, everything just tossed in. I wondered if it had been that way before Gary's boys sifted through it. At least I didn't have to worry that Robb would know I'd been pawing through his things. More unpaid bills and credit card receipts, most of the latter charges for necessities rather than luxuries made at gasoline stations, restaurants, and grocery stores. There were also three pawn tickets and a bank book marked *Account Closed.*

Next to the desk was a two-drawer file cabinet. In here the contents were organized and neatly labeled. A snap to find out that the Sannermans were up to their eyeballs in debt, that the house had a second mortgage which extracted every cent of equity, and that a thriving mutual fund had been decimated—all this taking place over the last eighteen months. This explained their bare-bones standard of living. A folder marked INSURANCE was even more interesting. It contained two term life insurance policies—$500,000 on Robb, $250,000 on Kate, mutual beneficiaries.

A quarter of a million dollars is not a fortune in this day and age, but lots of people have been killed for less by murderers who were not in Robb's dire financial straits. Gary must be jubilant. Robb had a motive, and, unless he had about fourteen witnesses who would swear he was out of town when his wife died, the man would soon be in very deep shit.

I padded out to the living room where Robb slept soundly on the sofa, feeling sorry for the poor bastard in spite of the doubts my scouting expedition had just added.

I left him to his nap and let myself out.

I'd waited too long to catch Elena. Just as I closed the door behind me, I saw her getting into an old green Chevy Nova. The car went past, a man driving, Elena beside him, her gaze meeting mine for a second, dark and impassive.

I walked over and rang Wylie's bell. Either he wasn't home or he simply wasn't answering the door. I gave up after a couple of rings and went to call him from the car phone. I got his machine, left a message, then tried his office. There, a machine offered voice mail. When I dialed Marilyn Wylie, I got something that sounded like Robbie the Robot advising me to leave my name and number. Desperate for human contact, I called Danny.

It was past quitting time, but my assistant had waited for me to check in. Messages included two from Gary who demanded that I present myself *muy pronto* for another grilling. Too late to return his call today.

Darn.

Danny gave me a quick rundown on Tamra. He had contacted all the hospitals in Orange, L.A., Riverside, and San Bernardino counties. Also the morgues. Nothing. She hadn't used her credit cards during the last three days or registered at local motels and hotels, at least not under her own name.

"You want me to widen the search?" Danny asked.

"I guess you'd better."

Danny had found a database covering places from San Diego to San Francisco. With automatic phone dialing it was still a daunting job.

When I asked if he'd received the information about Tamra's ATM card, he said he had spoken to Wylie earlier. The problem was that the account was in Tamra's name. Some "clerk type," as Wylie described him, had refused to give Wylie the information. Needless to say, my client was pretty ticked off.

"He says he'll speak to the manager, but it was too late to do it today," Danny said. "You want it legal or quick?"

"Jesus," I said. "I seriously think you ought to find yourself another job. I'm a bad influence."

"The worst," Danny agreed cheerfully. "What should I do?"

"Hold off and let me talk to Wylie. I'm going to try and convince him to bring in the police."

"This may help—Lee Gersky has a record."

Well, I'd seen Gersky's friends, so I can't say I was surprised. Mostly, Gersky had a problem with booze: a drunk and disorderly, two DUIs. However, the second time the highway patrol stopped him, Gersky took a swing at the officer, which got him an assault charge. This was pled down to resisting arrest; he was fined and paroled and lost his license.

I said, "I don't suppose you tracked down a current phone number or address?"

"Afraid not."

I passed along the two names of the 19D lease for background checks first thing the next day. Danny promised he would stay and continue calling hotels for Tamra while I hung out and waited for Wylie.

The sun was low enough so it was down behind Wylie's house. Although the van sat in that late afternoon shade, the temperature still hovered around a hundred degrees. A stakeout meant I could either sit and sweat or leave the engine and the air conditioner running and feel guilty about burning gas and polluting the air. I was saved from my eco-dilemma when a silver Mercedes cruised into the cul-de-sac with Wylie behind the wheel.

I met him on his driveway as one of three doors in the cavernous garage hummed open. He parked the car inside and got out, his face mirroring a combination of hope and dread.

"Have you found Tamra?"

"Not yet," I said. "But I've turned up some things we need to discuss."

He relaxed, believing, I suppose, that oldest of self-deceptive saws, the one about no news being a good thing.

"All right," he said. "Let's get out of this heat."

He led the way to his study and, once there, headed straight for the bar. This time I accepted his offer of a drink: a little vodka and lots of tonic and ice. While he sat behind his desk and sipped Glenlivet, I took the chair across from him and said, "Okay. First: we've checked out police records and hospitals in a four-county area. Nobody matching Tamra's description has been reported in an accident or as a victim of foul play."

No point in diluting his relief by adding that his daughter's body might be lying somewhere undiscovered, like Kate Sannerman's, a feast for the crows. I took a big swallow of my cold drink and outlined what I'd found out about Lee Gersky, including a description of his friends, a summary of his police record, and the fact that he seemed to have no visible means of support.

As I talked I could see Wylie's jaw setting and his thick eyebrows coming together in a scowl. I'd barely finished when he burst out, "Goddammit, you mean to tell me you're wasting time on Gersky? The guy's a loser. I could've told you that. Jesus Christ! You're supposed to be looking for my daughter. That's what I'm paying you to do, remember?"

"We're covering all the obvious angles," I said, aiming for reason and patience. "Hotels. Credit cards. Beyond that, it's standard investigative practice to talk to Tamra's friends. You gave me the impression she had broken up with Gersky. That's not what I'm hearing from other people. It seems logical to me that she'd at least tell her boyfriend where she was going, and it's even more likely she went to stay with him."

He didn't want to hear it. He slugged down the whiskey and stomped over to pour another shot.

Lord, I thought. Two drunken males in one day was definitely one too many.

"The problem is I can't find Gersky," I went on.

I was going to have to ask him for access to Tamra's room so I could look for an address book, notes, something that might lead me to the boyfriend, but I knew he would give me an automatic no unless I made a good case.

"He usually shares apartments with other people. That makes him hard to trace. If this was just a normal case of a young girl taking off in a snit, I'd be reassuring you that it was only a matter of time until I track him down, and when I did, probably I'd find Tamra with him. But Kate Sannerman's murder changes all that, Mr. Wylie. And she *was* murdered. That's official."

"This is ridiculous." He came to tower over me. "How many times do I have to tell you? It was a coincidence, that's all. What happened to Kate has nothing to do with Tamra. I don't like you harping on it, and I damn well don't like you trying to scare me."

"You're right," I said. "This time I *am* trying to scare you."

And succeeding. I recognize fear when I see it even when it's hidden beneath glowering bluster. He backed up and sat down abruptly on the overstuffed couch.

"Your daughter was a friend of Kate's," I said. "The Sannermans knew Gersky too. I don't know how well yet, but there was a connection. And I've found out enough about the guy to tell you he runs with a rough crowd and is handy with his fists."

"Good God, *Gersky?* You think he killed Kate?"

"I think he's a good suspect."

"You haven't told the police? They don't know about him?"

"Not yet."

"Because we had an understanding. I want this kept private, I told you that."

"And what about your daughter?"

"What about her?"

"If there's any possibility that Gersky's a murderer, do you really want Tamra with him?"

"You don't know that she is. You don't know anything for sure."

"I'm speculating," I admitted. "But I do have a basis for my suspicions. A strong enough one so I think we ought to go to the police. Wait," I said as he went red in the face and opened his mouth to interrupt. "In the first place I'm treading on some pretty thin legal ice here. I'm obligated to report anything I turn up that might be connected with Kate Sannerman's murder. *And,* I told you in the beginning that we could find Tamra faster if we filed a missing persons report."

"I can't believe this," Wylie said. "I hired you because I didn't want to deal with the police. I heard you were discreet. That you were good at your job. Seems to me, if you'd just stick to your work, Tamra'd be home and we wouldn't be having this conversation."

"Mr. Wylie—"

"Let me explain it again: we argued. My daughter went off in a huff. She's staying away so I'll worry about her. And I do. I want to know where she is. Then I can talk to her, we can straighten this out, and she can come home. Simple. All you have to do is *find* her. You do think you can do that?"

"I hope so."

At that moment I didn't want to tell him that people do vanish and are never found, or that if I did locate his daughter there was no way to predict whether she'd be living or dead.

"Just keep checking hotels," he ordered. "All the resorts. Tahoe. She went skiing there a couple of times."

"All right."

"The airports."

"Okay." I took a last sip of my drink. Most of the ice had melted, and it was flat and watery. "I think it might help if I had a look around her room again."

"Why?" he demanded.

I wasn't about to tell him my real reason, which was to look for something that might lead me to Gersky, so I said, "She might have jotted down a flight number or a place to stay."

That must have made sense, or else the two drinks on an empty stomach were dulling his natural belligerence. He said, "Oh, all right, go ahead," and stayed there, slouched down on the sofa, staring into his glass, while I went upstairs alone.

I guess Elena was observing Tamra's orders to stay out of the room. There was a coating of dust on the surfaces of the furniture, smudged here and there. Maybe Wylie had been up here himself and knew there was nothing to find. That's why he hadn't objected.

Sure enough my search yielded little: neatly folded underwear; lots of makeup, some of it barely used before it was pushed to the back of the drawer; a two-pound bag of M&Ms; a new sociology textbook with no notes in the margins, nothing highlighted or underlined; a Laguna Hills High yearbook with no autographs or ribald predictions and no picture of Tamra, just her name without any mention of activities or clubs.

The more I looked, the sadder I felt. Growing up I was a regular pack rat. I kept prizes from gumball machines, my first lost baby tooth nestled on cotton in a little gold earring box, desiccated bugs in a bottle. Books, old term papers, letters, pictures, birthday cards, programs, posters—my dad regularly issued dire warnings about fire hazards. I'd never been much for dolls, but I had a long-eared stuffed rabbit I got for Easter when I was two, the plush coat rubbed bare in spots and much mended, small neat stitches sewn by my mother before she died and ugly awkward stitches put in later by my dad. I still have it somewhere.

Maybe Tamra had boxed up all her personal things for storage. I really hoped she had, but I didn't think so, and the thought depressed me even more.

Lord, how I wished for a diary. Do young women even keep diaries these days? A journal, then. I checked between the mattress and box springs and other devious places just in case.

Nada.

I hate to admit it, but I even used a pencil on the memo pad next to her phone to see if she'd made an important note. Hey, it works on TV, but all the effort got me was some paper shaded in graphite gray.

Finally, in one of the three shoulder bags in the closet I found a packaged condom and a couple of photographs. If Wylie had conducted his own search, maybe he hadn't thought about delving into the purses. Well, who was the professional here anyway?

Both photos had been taken in the Sannermans' back yard. One was of the palomino, Goldy. In the other, Tamra in jeans and a T-shirt and Kate in a bathing suit sat on the patio while a young fellow leaned down between them, a hand on the back of each chair. He wore jeans like Tamra but no shirt. I had a damn good idea who he was.

Something about him reminded me of his ex-roommates, especially Bix, maybe the muscular shoulders and slightly Neanderthal shape of the head. Steroids came to mind. Which might explain the violent temper. He had dark hair, thick and rough, down to his shoulders and was good-looking in a sly, brutish sort of way. No wonder Wylie went into denial at the thought of Lee Gersky with his little girl.

Tamra leaned back, touching Gersky's arm, and looked straight into the camera, her mouth relaxed in the ghost of a smile but the big eyes darkly serious. Kate sat forward in her chair, laughing, looking as though she was about to spring up and pounce on the person taking the picture—Robb, or so I assumed.

I went back downstairs, hoping I'd find Wylie sloshed and out cold on the sofa just like Robb, but no such luck. Although his color was a little high, Wylie was at his desk, plenty sober enough and not at all surprised when I said I hadn't found anything in Tamra's room. Since the picture he kept on his desk was the one that showed Tamra at about age two, somehow I didn't think he'd be reassured by the news that his daughter practiced safe sex. And I didn't tell him about the photo I had tucked away in my handbag.

If Benjamin Wylie wasn't the most obstinate man I'd ever met, he came close. Nothing I said about Gersky, or the murder, or my intuition about the danger his daughter was in was going to make him change his mind.

I was more certain than ever that he was hiding something from me. To tell the truth I might have suspected Wylie had murdered Kate himself with his daughter as witness except I thought he was one of those men who might rant and rave but could never be truly ruled by passion.

I just said I'd be in touch, and he said fine, and I went out into the bright, hot twilight.

On the drive home, I told myself that although Wylie was cranky and pigheaded, he was still the guy who was paying my hourly fee plus expenses. Does the client who acts like a jackass deserve as much loyalty as the one who is a prince of a fellow? So I didn't like him; hell, if I wanted to be around nice, likeable people, I'd get another profession. I owed it to him to do the job the way he wanted it done.

Didn't I?

Soon after I arrived at my apartment, Danny called to say that so far his hotel search was coming up goose eggs. He was knocking off for the night and would try again tomorrow. And did I remember about Gary Hofer?

How could I forget?

Like it or not I was going to have to talk to Gary tomorrow, and I had to decide what to tell him.

I decided I'd sleep on it.

I slept.

In the morning I still didn't know what to do.

EIGHT

ONE THING ABOUT being so preoccupied, at least I'd stopped brooding about my social life. And, come to think of it, Erik hadn't called to remind me about our lunch date. I'd give him points for that. On the other hand, maybe he'd forgotten all about it just like I had.

After my fast morning walk and a shower, I figured there was no sense putting off the inevitable. I'd better go see Gary Hofer before he sent out a squad car. So I dressed in my power suit—a charcoal pinstripe, $199.99 on sale at Nordstrom's—surveyed myself in the mirror, and thought *What the hell*. Gary would not be impressed no matter what I wore, and it was already hot at seven A.M.

I changed to white, wrinkled cotton slacks—they were *meant* to be wrinkled, my kind of clothes—and a turquoise knit top, slipped on some sandals, and headed for the Orange County Sheriff-Coroner's Department—to give it its full name. Since Mom's Kountry Kooking was right on the way, I stopped for a quick breakfast, but I still made it to the department's headquarters on Flower Street shortly after eight.

As far as I could see there didn't seem to be a whole lot going on in the Investigative Unit, but Gary let me cool my heels until nine. You leave a civilian waiting because nothing unnerves the ordinary citizen more than sitting and feeling surrounded by the inexorable grinding of the wheels of justice. With me, Gary had to know that waiting's part of my job and I'm not intimidated easily. I classified his delay as simply an exercise in muscle flexing.

While his little display of authority didn't bother me, it did provide the opportunity to go over my moral dilemma a few more times. Which was: to whom did I owe my allegiance, my client or his daughter, whose life might be endangered by my silence?

By the time I was summoned into Gary's inner sanctum, I think I knew what I had to do. Still, I wasn't going to make it easy for him. Or maybe I just had to do a little muscle flexing of my own.

Gary's office was the bland functional cubicle that government does best, with a metal desk and file cabinet and commercial-grade carpeting, sort of a mottled orange and brown, the kind that's not supposed to show dirt and wear but always does.

Decorating options are at a minimum in a place like that. Gary had done what he could by covering the institutional-beige walls with framed photos and plaques. Naturally, the subject of this array was Gary himself: graduation from the Police Academy (look closely and you might see me somewhere in the background); handshaking ceremonies over the years with then Mayor Bradley, several L.A. county supervisors, and a couple of movie stars, including the great Duke himself, John Wayne. No wonder Gary had immigrated to Orange County.

"Nice that you found some time in your schedule to fit me in," he said.

He remained seated behind his desk. He was wearing a charcoal pinstripe—I swear—although his looked like it cost at least a thousand dollars more than mine. Another photo on his desk proved that he did occasionally wear casual clothes. Somewhere at a marina in front of a sleek-looking boat named *Sunni's Delight*, wearing white slacks and a blue open-necked shirt, he posed with a cute little blonde in a pink sundress, the two of them flashing identical dazzling smiles.

A cream-colored shirt and a marginally gaudy tie completed his current ensemble. Better him than me. Either the air conditioning was on the fritz or the county was cutting costs by bumping up the thermostat. Gary's thinning hairline was already damp with sweat.

He hadn't invited me to sit down, but I pulled up a chair anyway.

I said, "I was pretty busy yesterday."

"With your job for Mr. Wylie."

"With that one," I agreed.

He had my statement in front of him. He folded his hands on top of it, soft hands with manicured nails. "One thing before we start. I don't show any favoritism here. Just because we were once—" he searched for the term, discarding, I presume, best buddies "—fellow officers, that doesn't mean squat when it comes to a homicide case. You have no official standing. Zero."

A few months ago I was sure his tone would have been a lot different, back when Erik was smoothing the bumps out of my life. Gary is, if nothing else, acutely attuned to the force field of power and influence.

Now he went on, "You get down here when I tell you to, and once you're here I expect your full cooperation."

"Would you like anything else?" I asked politely. "Blood? Bone marrow?"

"Oh, cut the shit," he said, baring his pearly whites. "I know you're looking for Tamra Wylie. If there's any connection between this girl and Kate Sannerman's murder, I want to know about it right now."

So he'd found out what I was doing for Wylie. No surprise. Elena's reticence might have vanished if faced with an official questioning. Or Robb might have sobered up long enough to blab. Wylie would blame me in any case.

Now what?

I could stall and tell half truths. I've done it before. Hell, I've outright *lied* when I felt lying was justified. Besides, discussing a case with a cop went against the grain, it really did, especially with Gary.

This time, however, I had to weigh something more than ethics or personal bias or a job. What I had to put on the scale was my unshakable feeling that Tamra might be in a lot of trouble, that she needed to be found as soon as possible, and that the police were better equipped to find her than I was.

So I told Gary everything. Well, almost everything. I didn't change my story about finding Kate's body; I didn't describe my foray through the Sannermans' house after I talked to Robb last night; and I didn't pass along the photo of Tamra, Lee, and Kate. All of these involved explanations I wasn't ready to give to old by-the-book Gary. I did tell him about Lee Gersky and the time element, and I emphasized Gersky's background.

When I finished he said, "That's it then? You're sure?"

"That's it."

"Okay." He reached for the phone. "I'll have somebody take your statement."

"Wait a minute." I hadn't expected unbridled excitement, but I had thought I'd get a flicker of interest. "What are you going to do? Are you going to look for Tamra?"

"I can't discuss an ongoing investigation, Delilah," he said with a touch of smug self-righteousness. "You know that."

"Well, give me a hint. My client's not going to be real happy about this."

Gary's patronizing smirk told me I deserved whatever I got, caving in the way I had. "Can't do it. Sorry."

I jumped up, resisting the urge to smash my chair over his head.

"Yeah, you're that," I said, "and an ass as well, but you're not stupid, and I figure you're going to think about Tamra Wylie and Lee Gersky as material witnesses and get out an APB because if you don't and anything happens to Tamra, I'm going to make such a stink you'll wish you'd stayed the hell in L.A."

I left him with his mouth open, but I did resist slamming the door behind me.

Real control.

By the time I'd given my statement and was on my way to my office, depression and doubts moved in. My threats might encourage Gary to do *something*, but I didn't flatter myself that he'd be moving with any urgency. And, once I called Wylie, I was pretty sure I wouldn't be looking for Tamra anymore.

As soon as I walked in the door, Danny said, "You went to the police."

"That wasn't a question. How'd you know?"

"Benjamin Wylie called."

"And?"

"He said the police called him."

"And?"

"He said to tell you you're fired."

THERE WAS A BIT MORE to Wylie's message. If the retainer he'd given me didn't cover my time and expenses, tough. That's all I was getting.

I tried to phone him back, but the machine answered. I left a message explaining that the police were probably looking for Tamra but urging him to hire another PI and offering a couple of suggestions, although my recommendation was likely to be a guarantee that neither would be hired as a replacement.

Danny had just talked to the bank about Tamra's account. Apparently, Wylie had convinced them to cooperate and give us access to Tamra's ATM transactions; approximately two-thirds of the hotels and motels outside Orange County remained to be contacted. Not to mention the follow-up interviews I had planned.

"Bloody *hell*," I muttered, wondering how I could ever have thought that handing my case over to Gary Hofer was the right thing to do.

Well, I had.

And that was that.

After we finished up the paperwork, I gave Danny the rest of the day off. I returned a few phone calls, but most of this was old business. There was not a new client in sight. I paid a few bills and figured my bank balance. No reason to panic—yet.

I had one errand to run: over to the gun shop to pick up the Beretta. Then I went to the pistol range in Orange to fire a few practice rounds—and a good thing, too. There were two ways to chamber the first cartridge into firing position: you could pull the slide or flip up a little door on the barrel and insert a cartridge directly. I discovered right away that the slide took a lot more strength than I remembered from the gun shop. I opted for one in the barrel—with the safety on, of course, until I was ready to use it.

On the range the little gun sounded like a pea-shooter compared to the .44 Magnum blasting away a couple of stalls down, but it was as advertised: fairly accurate at close range and easily concealed. After I took the Beretta home and cleaned and reloaded it, I locked it in the van's glove box with my .38.

Get myself an Uzi and I'd have a regular arsenal.

I considered a workout. God knows I needed one, but I knew Rita would want to talk about Erik. I was trying very hard not to even *think* about Erik and our lunch tomorrow. Which I could still skip—I had not totally ruled out that option.

Instead of going to the gym, I stopped at my apartment, changed to shorts and a tank top, and drove to Laguna. The summer tourists were gone, but there were plenty of locals taking advantage of the bright sunlight and the warm water. I parked at the south end of town down on Cleo Street and walked all the way up along the beach as far as I could go, clambering over rocks in places, and ending up in Heisler Park on the asphalt path that follows the edge of the cliffs.

Where the park ended at the walls of the gated community of Emerald Bay, I turned around and headed back. The breeze off the ocean took the sizzle out of the heat, tempering the air, coming as close to creating a perfect day as possible in a world of smog and ever increasing pollution.

By the time I hiked back to the Hotel Laguna, I was starved. I drank half a liter of Chardonnay and ate Chinese chicken salad out on the terrace, listening to the shrieks of gulls and the happy cries of children playing in the surf.

The breeze developed a sharp, salty edge while I lingered there, so I went to the van for a sweatshirt. Then I sat on the sand with my back up against the smooth warmth of a sandstone boulder and watched the sun go down.

I remembered...

Sitting on the beach between the fork of Jack's legs, my back snuggled against him, his arms wrapped around me, perfectly content...

The sweet snippet of memory was fresh and whole, followed by a moment of loss as devastating as it had ever been. But if time didn't heal completely, it did pile up scar tissue, so the moment passed quickly.

Some animals mate for life. Swans and prairie voles do; some people, too. I thought for a while maybe I was one of those people. But I don't think so anymore. And to tell the truth I was getting damn sick of eating and watching sunsets alone.

I wanted somebody in my life. Maybe not Erik, *surely* not him, but if not, well, I needed to find that out, get the man out of my system, and move on.

Simple.

Just go have the damn lunch with him tomorrow and see how it went. So why did I feel like I was up on one of those cliffs in Heisler Park about to jump into the rocky ocean and be swept out to sea?

NINE

INLAND, the offshore flow of the week's Santa Ana winds had bottled up the air in the basin and turned it into sulfurous yellow-brown muck, but the Balboa peninsula in Newport Beach had its own microclimate with soft blue skies and enough of a sea breeze to snap the sails of a little catamaran that wove its way through the larger, more expensive traffic on the bay.

I arrived at the Harborside restaurant fashionably late because I'd miscalculated the number of people heading for the beach, and then, once across the bridge over the Lido channel, I'd been forced to circle the Marina Village parking structure twice.

A beautiful young woman in a tropical print blouse and a sarong assured me that Erik was already there and waiting. I could tell she knew who he was. Hell, a lot of people in Orange County do, especially the upscale part of the population living in Newport Beach. The man has a high-recognition value what with his name being plastered on development projects all over the place these past twenty years as well as in the society column.

The hostess was also sizing me up with a veiled expression that generated a sudden urge to find a mirror. I muttered something about a quick trip to the ladies' room and hurried off.

I'd changed clothes three times that morning, finally settling on a cotton gauze skirt and a V-neck top that knotted at the shoulders, both in something the tag called dark jungle green.

Big mistake.

I realized that the color gave my brown eyes a peculiar yellow cast and made my skin look like I'd just recovered from a bout of jaundice. My hair was not growing out of the short cut nearly fast enough. It had been particularly unruly that morning, and the ton of gel I'd applied hadn't tamed the spikes. All it had done was solidify. I'd chewed off my lipstick, and now I discovered I hadn't returned the tube to my bag.

And the earrings—I'd never planned to have a piercing done. However, a few months back a very nasty guy—one of the two who bombed my office—forcibly did the job on the right lobe with a fishing lure. So, what the hell, I figured I might as well do the left one the more conventional way. The thing is, once you have the holes, you have to fill them, and I find myself buying unusual and impractical baubles. Usually these wind up in a drawer because most of the time I wear gold studs. Not today. Big hoops dangled just above my shoulders, looking like something only a gypsy fortune-teller would wear.

Oh well, not much I could do except pat my stiff hair and take my tasteless, messy self out to have lunch with the most eligible bachelor in Orange County.

He waited for me on the patio overlooking the bay, lean and tan and wearing a silky blue shirt that matched his eyes and pressed, white Dockers. His sleeves were turned up to reveal a Patek Philippe watch. I'd recovered a watch like that for a client once, very plain, solid gold—and worth twenty thousand bucks.

He smiled and said, "I was beginning to think you'd stood me up."

"Traffic," I explained and smiled back, took a menu from the hostess and smiled at her too—well, really a grin that said *Eat your heart out.*

"I ordered some wine." Erik indicated one of those silver buckets on a stand next to the table, and almost magically a waiter appeared, a young guy in shorts and a safari shirt, barely old enough to drink booze let alone serve it. "But if you'd like something else—"

"No, that's fine."

The waiter poured. A French label—even the bottle looked expensive. The stuff tasted a little tart to me, but what do I know? When I want to splurge I buy an obscure northern California vintage on special at Trader Joe's. Then the waiter said he was Josh and regaled us with the specials and the list of fresh fish in the kind of confident voice that told me he was just working here to kill some time and in a year or so he'd be brokering stock deals in between sailing and tennis.

"Give us a minute," Erik said.

"No, I'm starved, let's order," I said and asked for sea bass, sounding crisp and decisive when in fact it was the only thing I remembered from Josh's recitation.

Erik ordered shark and Josh left us alone for a few seconds. We had the best table, of course, in a spot with the most privacy the patio had to offer, shaded by a lush stand of banana and bamboo. I ate some bread sticks because I really was hungry. I'd skipped breakfast what with all the time I'd spent on wardrobe selection. Erik sipped his wine and watched me over the rim of the glass. I began to think maybe the jungle green outfit and the earrings weren't a mistake after all.

"How's our case going?" he asked.

"I don't have a case anymore. I was fired."

"Fired? I can't believe that." There was a protective, incredulous edge in his voice that I liked.

"The client had a right," I said. "I didn't do what he wanted."

"Well, maybe he should have listened. You do excellent work."

It occurred to me then that mostly what Erik and I knew about each other came from dossiers. Back when he'd tried to hire me for his private security staff, more to distract me from the case I was on rather than because he valued my talent, I was sure Charlie Colfax had provided him a complete background. And Charlie was the man to do it. Besides running the largest private investigation firm in Orange County, he'd known Jack before Jack and I were married, long before we'd opened our own agency.

Since then I've put together a pretty complete folder on Erik, too. As I've confessed, I'm a snoop; I also wanted to know all about the man who refused to get out of my life, who made sure I got on my feet financially by referring the moneyed people to me, who personally saw to it I had the best medical care money could buy when I wound up in the hospital a few months back after the bombing.

My research told me that his father had made a small fortune building homes for veterans returning from World War II, but that it was Erik who had made the real money with the housing tracts, condos, and commercial buildings that covered Orange County. More facts: he'd been married twice, and he had a seventeen-year-old daughter, Nicole, by his first wife. Nicole had moved back East with her mother; she was just starting her first year at Vassar.

I thought about asking him for some firsthand insight into Benjamin Wylie's relationship with Tamra; it was a perfect opening, a way to delve into Erik's personal life, but the truth is I just didn't want to play detective. I was content to enjoy the feel of sunlight slanting down through the leaves, to savor the wine, which was tasting better all the time, and to let Erik steer the conversation.

He was so good at it, by the time we finished our salads, we were talking about everything...and nothing. Exactly the kind of low-key conversation people have in a place like that.

I realized I wasn't going to add one fact or statistic to my file on Erik, but I was going to retain a hundred sensory memories: the slight charcoal taste of the fish and the honeyed sweetness of melon, the texture of the starched linen napkins, the sheen of Erik's shirt and the way it slid over his shoulders when he moved.

Well, yes, I was a little drunk, but I didn't mind at all and was disappointed when Josh cleared the dishes, took away the empty wine bottles, and brought coffee. I even let Erik accept the bill and hand Josh a credit card, a tacit admission that the lunch had been, after all, a date.

"I know it's short notice," Erik said, "but I have to go to a dinner tomorrow night, a benefit for the symphony. I'd like you to go with me."

Dressy, I'd bet. Probably black-tie. He'd pick me up in the limo. Well, we've all seen what happens in limos in the movies. Or he'd suggest we go by his house afterward for a drink, and one thing would lead to another.

I'm not sure if it was the inevitability of it all that sent me into a panic or the fact that I'd seen Erik in a tux and there was not one thing in my closet, probably not one thing in South Coast Plaza, that would make me feel like I belonged on his arm.

"Tomorrow?" I said. "Gee, sorry. Not tomorrow. I can't."

The way he looked at me I thought I hadn't fooled him for a second. Taking me off the hook, he said, "Okay. One other night next week, then. I'll call you."

I didn't say yes, but I didn't say no either. Walking away from the table through the restaurant I was struck by the thought that as soon as I quit saying no, he might lose interest, that it could very well be the thrill of the chase that kept him coming back, and Lord knows I'd led him a merry one.

While this was running through my mind, we had walked back out to the hostess section. A couple stood there, waiting. Weird how when you suddenly see somebody you know in a setting that's out of context, you have to readjust your mind-set before you truly recognize them.

I knew the man all right. It was Gary Hofer, looking as bemused as I was, and the woman was the blonde from the picture on his desk. Petite, winsome, pert—all words that might have been coined just for her.

She gave a big smile of recognition and said, "Oh, *Erik,* hello."

Erik said, "Hi, Sunni," and the two of them did a quick kissy-face routine.

"Darling, this is Erik Lundstrom," she said to Gary. "Erik, my husband, Gary Hofer."

It clicked then. *Sunni's Delight,* the mini-yacht in the picture, was not just background; Gary's sudden move to Orange County, the fancy duds, and a general sense of moving up in the world—now it made sense. His wife moved in Erik's circles, so imagine the dowry.

Gary was going through a confused reevaluation of his own, seeing me there with Erik. And, believe me, Gary would know all about Erik. Well, I admit it. I was not above tucking my hand in Erik's arm just to make sure Gary didn't write this off as "desperate PI wooing a client."

This ploy got me a puzzled look from Erik, but I noticed he followed my lead, covering my hand with his, intimate and possessive, as he introduced us.

"Nice to meet you, Sunni," I said. "Hi, Gary. Gary and I go a long way back."

"You know each other?" Sunni asked.

"Delilah and I are old friends," Gary declared, his recent condescension and harassment obviously forgotten, not so by-the-book after all. "We've been working on a case together. I put out that APB, Delilah. I don't think you really have to worry about your girl, though. We're getting ready to make an arrest."

And I'd bet it was Robb Sannerman who was going in the slammer.

The saronged hostess came with her menus to say their table was ready.

"You two don't have to run off, do you?" Sunni asked. "We spent the morning on the water and we're famished, but, please, sit down with us and visit."

"Gee, sorry," I said. "We can't. Maybe some other time."

After goodbye noises Erik and I left the restaurant arm in arm, my discomfort level rising with every step. As soon as we were out of Gary's line of sight, I pulled away, fumbling in my purse for my sunglasses and feeling color rise in my cheeks.

"Listen," I said, "I can explain—I mean—about acting like we—you know. The man is such a slime, and—anyway, you already know I'm not above—well—*using* situations—and people—when I have to."

We had stopped under one of those tree-size birds of paradise, and he just stood there, looking bemused, perfectly content to let me put both feet in my mouth.

"Oh, hell," I said. "I won't make excuses. If you insist on hanging around with me, you might as well get used to it."

"Okay, I'll accept that," he said with a grin. "On one condition." He offered his arm. "One stroll up and down the boardwalk."

I hesitated. "We'll walk past the patio and wave to Gary and Sunni."

"Deal," he said.

TEN

I WAS BARELY IN THE DOOR of my apartment when Rita called.

"Well, did you go?" she asked.

"Yeah, I went."

"And?"

"It was nice," I said.

"You didn't pick a fight? You actually sat there and ate and talked and everything?"

"Believe it or not."

"Then what happened?"

"Nothing."

"He asked you out again," she said. "Are you going?"

"I don't know. Maybe. I guess so."

"Go."

"It's never going to work, Rita."

"You'd be surprised. Look at Farley and me."

"I'm afraid my problem with Erik is a little more basic."

"What could be more basic than learning to eat sprouts and tofu? Just do it, kiddo. Don't think about it too much; don't analyze it to death."

I promised I'd try, but after I hung up, I realized I was doing just that: analyzing. I couldn't help it. It's my nature to pick things apart.

Lunch had been nice, it had been wonderful, so how come it bothered me so much? Cinderella didn't go into a moral dither when she was invited to the ball, did she? Look at Gary. He had no trouble making the adjustment. Well, Gary wouldn't. And plenty of women would kill for a wealthy guy with a white-horse mentality, and never mind feminist concerns.

But not me.

Maybe my roots were buried way back in the mountains of West Virginia where my mother had been born, in rocky soil that yielded only coal and misery. I'm suspicious of things that come too easily. And wealth is seductive. I could feel that already, and it scared me. So easy to lose yourself, to wake up one day and find you don't know who you are anymore.

And look at the way I'd used Erik today. I mean, true, my main purpose had just been to needle Gary. Easy enough to start using the relationship for pressuring tactics. In a sense, even now, wasn't I just as bad as social-climbing Gary?

I wandered around the apartment, at loose ends, examining my motives and probing my ethics for a good part of the afternoon before deciding that my time was better spent doing the laundry and chasing some dust bunnies.

Once started, I launched into a full-scale cleaning job, not a major project since the apartment is small. One bedroom, a tiny kitchen—the whole place could be tucked into a corner of Erik's sprawling house.

The furniture is a hodge-podge; I buy for comfort and keep things forever, sticking to neutral browns and beiges—apartment colors—and a good thing because I've bounded around a lot since Jack died.

I do own one original painting, given to me by a grateful client, her work, surprisingly good for an amateur: Matilija poppies, huge and papery white against gray-green leaves. Otherwise, I have a couple of seascape prints I use to cover dings and gouges in the plasterboard. These are not in the same league as Erik's Picasso and Monets, of course.

Oh, hell.

Erik again.

Grateful to escape my thoughts, I went over to the Sanchezes early for dinner with Jorge, Consuelo, and the kids. I sidestepped their well-intentioned questions about my personal life by playing hearts with the youngest, Isabel, until the rest of the kitchen staff from Mom's arrived for our poker game.

Good thing I didn't need my winnings to eke out my income. At midnight, down fifty dollars, I decided it was time to go home.

Next morning Rita and Farley persuaded me to go out for brunch. "Something healthy for a change," Rita said, so I knew I was in for crunchy textures and lots of greenery. Rita suggested I call Erik and ask him to come along, an idea I firmly squelched.

We ate in a new place down on Lake Mission Viejo, so at least the view was nice. Artificial, but nice. Well, water's water, even if the lake is man-made. A shame we couldn't see the mountains because of the smog.

Leaving the restaurant, I remembered to do a routine check of the answering machine at the office. Robb Sannerman had left a message, sounding cold sober and shaky on the tape, saying he needed to talk to me. It was urgent.

I called him back, a little surprised he was still at home and not in jail. He apologized for passing out on me the other night, then said, "You told me you were looking for Tamra, that she left about the same time Kate was killed. It hit me this morning. Maybe she saw something. Do you think that's possible?"

"Could be."

"God, I hope so. Have you had any luck finding her?"

"No," I said, "and I'm afraid I'm not looking for her anymore."

"Why not?"

"Mr. Wylie and I had a parting of the ways."

"Oh, Jesus," he said in despair. "I was hoping— listen, I'm going to be arrested. I know it. I just got home from Santa Ana. The police questioned me for hours. I told them about Tamra but they just blew it off."

"There is an APB out on her and Lee," I said.

"Lee? What's he got to do with it?"

"I thought maybe Tamra was with him," I said, keeping the rest of my suspicions to myself. I was curious about Robb's reaction the other night when I first mentioned Gersky's name, but now didn't seem the time to bring it up.

"Do you really think the police are going to try to find them?" Robb asked. "Why should they? They've got me. Please, Delilah, can you come down here? I need some help."

"What you need is a good attorney."

"Maybe I do, but I need you, too. At least come and talk to me."

I sighed. I'd just begun to accept that I was out of the case. Did I really want back in? Still, it was a short drive over to Nellie Gail and the man was desperate, so finally I said I'd come but only if he got in touch

with an attorney, and I gave him two recommenda-
tions.

Then I called Danny at home to tell him what was
happening and ask him to stand by. He promised to go
into the office if I needed him.

Ten minutes later I parked on the Sannermans'
driveway, wondering if Wylie would see me there and
not caring much if he did. Around the side of the
house a leftover remnant of yellow crime scene tape
still hung on the gate; the crows were off looking for
fresh pickings.

An involuntary shiver rippled my back as I remembered opening that gate four days ago. I put the scene
out of my mind, went up to the front door, and rang
the bell.

Robb answered so quickly, I think he must have
been watching for me. Haggard and drawn, he looked
like he'd aged ten years in the past few days. He ush-
ered me in, apologizing again, urging me to sit down,
offering me a drink and assuring me he wouldn't have
any, that he intended to stay sober, both pathetically
grateful that I was there and ashamed of his predica-
ment.

"Let's have some coffee," I said. "I'll make it. You
just sit."

"Okay, but I think you'll have to open a fresh can—
in the pantry."

"Oh, don't worry, I'm sure I can find everything."

That part was easy, of course, after I'd rummaged
through the cupboards the other day. In the kitchen,
the counter looked messier than ever. More mail had
been piled on the breakfast bar, added to the letters

from the last time I'd been here. There were dishes in the sink.

While the coffee dripped, I scrounged up some cookies, figuring it couldn't hurt to get his blood sugar up. I carried two mugs, the cookie plate, spoons, a bowl with packets of creamer and sweetener, and some napkins out to the family room. No tray. Well, I'd had a lot of practice back when I used to moonlight at Mom's.

Slumped down on the couch, he shook his head at the cookies, then huddled over his mug as though it was the dead of winter and he needed warmth.

"I retained one of the lawyers you suggested," he said. "Leah Bennett. She told me to call when they serve the arrest warrant. *Jesus,* I can't believe this is happening. You have to find Tamra for me."

"You're counting way too heavily on that, Robb. There's no guarantee she saw anything."

"If she didn't, can't you find somebody—a witness? Good Christ, find the person who really did this."

"You didn't kill her?" I meant it to be blunt.

"No," he said. "Please, you've got to believe me. Kate and I—we had problems. We were ready to split up, but I wouldn't—my God, you saw her. I couldn't do something like that."

The prisons are full of people who will look you straight in the eye and tell you no way was it their fingerprints on the gun, their sperm, their blood, their hair. Eyewitnesses? Surveillance tapes? Lab tests? Don't care, man, I was *framed.*

Still, while Robb might lie, I had to ask. Sometimes you can read it in the eyes. Robb's were big, brown, and terror-filled. The trick was judging whether that terror came from being falsely accused or just being caught.

I said, "Tell me about the problems you were having with your wife."

He gripped the mug in both hands and stared down into the coffee. "Things had just gone wrong, so wrong, and I wasn't sure there was anything we could do to make them right again."

"What things?" I persisted, but the doorbell rang, startling Robb so he sloshed coffee from the mug.

"Are you expecting someone?" I asked.

"No. Do you think it's—oh, God—it's *them.*" He sat, frozen, coffee running down his arm. And no doubt about who he thought was ringing the bell.

"Stay calm." I took the mug from his hand and gave him a napkin. "I'll get it."

I wasn't surprised to find two uniformed police officers at the door, but I hadn't expected Gary. I figured the press couldn't be far behind. Why else would Gary be here on a Sunday instead of cruising around Newport harbor on *Sunni's Delight.* Officially, only the public relations officer does the talking for the department, but, hey, if the TV cameras happen to catch the man who solved the case and he's personally escorting a deranged murderer to the squad car, what can it hurt?

"Delilah?" Gary said, like maybe he was getting peeved at me for popping up unexpectedly all the time. "What are you doing here?"

"Mr Sannerman wants to retain me to assist his attorney. He thought you might be stopping by."

"Where is he?"

I led them into the family room where Robb had slumped even lower on the couch as though his very bones were softening and losing shape.

Gary stopped in the doorway and waved the two uniforms on in to do the formalities. Meanwhile, Gary was asking me about Wylie and I told him my status with my ex-client.

"Well," Gary said, "we've been friends too long, so I've got to say I really think you ought to back out of this one, Delilah."

The cops were putting the cuffs on Robb, and Robb was saying, "I told you I want to call my lawyer. You said I could and I want to call her," his voice rising in panic.

"Gary, come on," I said. "I'll just do it for him; you won't be buying anything by making him wait."

He considered, a flicker of resentment in his eyes; told the cop, "Let him make the call." Then to me: "You're making a big mistake here. Sannerman's going down."

"You're sure of that?"

"Oh yeah." My old pal lowered his voice. "I'm jumping the gun telling you this, but it'll all come out in discovery anyway. Sannerman told us he was out of town the day his wife died, but guess what? According to American West Airlines, he came in from Phoenix at 2:02 P.M. and went back at 4:55. He was here, Delilah. We got him nailed."

GARY'S NEWFOUND generosity only went so far. He wouldn't let me talk to Robb. If I was fool enough to work for the guy, I could visit him in jail after the booking procedure. I made a quick dash through the rapidly forming media gauntlet outside Robb's house, got in my van, and headed for the freeway. The drive north gave me plenty of time to think because traffic was already down to a crawl, the road jammed with weekenders returning home.

And what I thought was, Gary was probably right. I ought to back away. Just on a practical level, I knew there was a chance Robb wouldn't be able to pay me—unless Leah Bennett and I got him off so he could collect the insurance, and now, according to Gary, Robb not only had a reason to kill Kate, he'd been right here in Orange County on the day she died.

Still, even before I inched my way past the El Toro Y, I knew I was going to take the case. Maybe it was some primal revulsion at the memory of Kate's body, not only brutalized but left like carrion, or the nagging feel of wanting to know what happened—not the police's version, the real truth. It could even have been the memory of Robb's puppy-dog eyes.

One thing for sure: I wasn't about to let Gary tell me what I should do.

So I called Danny from the car phone and told him to go on over to the office and pick up where he'd left off. Then I went home for a change of clothes and a sandwich.

I was on my way to the Orange County jail when I remembered that I could have been hanging out with the beautiful people tonight, eating a fancy dinner, having hot sex with Erik in a limo.

Not my kind of evening.

Except maybe for that last part.

ELEVEN

ROBB LOOKED SHRUNKEN and pale inside a standard-issue orange jumpsuit, as though he'd already been inside long enough to acquire a jail-house pallor. We sat on hard, straight-back chairs in a small dismal room that smelled of Lysol, the application not strong enough to cover the odor of stale cigarettes. I'd brought along two containers of coffee, but Robb shook his head at the offer.

"You saw Leah?" I asked.

His nod was a jerky up-and-down movement. "She said I have to stay here until the arraignment. That maybe I won't get out at all if the bail is too high. The judge won't do that, will he? I'm not a criminal. I've never had more than a couple of traffic tickets."

"The court will take that into consideration." Along with the brutal nature of the murder and the ease of his jumping on a plane and flying off to South America, although I figured he didn't want to hear that, so I just said, "Leah's good at her job. You'll have to trust her to do the best she can. And you have to trust me, too, Robb. No holding back."

Another nod and dumb, animal-level misery in his eyes.

I just waited, took the lid off my coffee, and sipped. He certainly wasn't going anywhere.

"Hofer knows, doesn't he?" Robb asked finally. "That I was here the day Kate died?"

"Yes, he does."

"I knew he'd find out. I should have told him right away. But it scared hell out of me, the kinds of questions he was asking, and I *was* out of town. So that's what I said, and then I couldn't admit I hadn't told the whole truth. It was so stupid. But I bought the ticket to fly back here under my own name. I wouldn't do that if I was going to kill somebody, would I?"

"Robb, most murders are not brilliantly planned, no matter what you read. Cops keep their clearance rates up because killers do stupid things. Now, was Kate alive when you got home?"

"I didn't go home. My God, if I had, maybe I'd've been there, and whoever killed her—well, it couldn't have happened." His voice shook and he had to make a visible effort to regain control.

"The meetings in Phoenix—I went over Sunday night because they started first thing Monday morning, but we finished early that day. I'd been thinking about Kate. Things were getting so bad, it was *all* I could think about. I couldn't concentrate on work. I design computer systems—networks—you just can't screw it up. Jesus, I was lucky they didn't fire me. They probably will now.

"I decided I had to talk to Kate, to settle things once and for all. I flew back. I got my car out of the lot at the airport. But then, all I did was drive around. I don't know—it was like I'd expended all this energy getting here, I just felt drained and paralyzed. And I wasn't even sure I was doing the right thing, that I really knew what I wanted to say to Kate."

I could sympathize with his indecision. I know the feelings well.

"So I drove back to the airport," he said, "and got the next flight to Phoenix."

"While you were here, where did you go?"

"I don't know. Just around. I went south on the freeway, but I went right on past my exit. I think I got off at Crown Valley, but I'm not sure."

"Did you stop for gas?"

"No."

"A drink? Something to eat? To use the bathroom?"

He shook his head and kept shaking it.

"Don't they have to prove I was there at the house?" he asked. "I mean, my God, don't they have to really *prove it?*"

"Ask Leah," I advised, and I didn't envy her explaining about the weight of circumstantial evidence. "What I want you to do: Go back over that afternoon. Write it all down. Every single thing you did. Maybe you'll remember something."

He promised he would, looking more hopeful than he should have.

"All right," I said, "now I want to hear about you and Kate."

"It's hard to—" He reached for his coffee, took off the lid, stared at the steam wafting up. "I didn't tell the cops. Leah said that was good, that I shouldn't say anything."

"Then do what Leah says. But tell me."

He took a couple of gulps of coffee. "I still can't believe everything would go so wrong. Three years ago, when we bought the house, we were on top of the world. Kate was in real estate. She was good at it, too, making money even with the economy so tight. She got us a good deal on the house. We had money in the bank, some investments. Then it all went to hell. And it was my fault.''

He put the coffee down and jumped up to pace around the small, windowless room.

"There was a party, over in Laguna Beach. This was almost two years ago. Some people from a company in Irvine, I'd set up their computer system, couple of young guys, lots of money. Kate didn't even want to go. She thought it would be boring. But it was a great party, a real blast," he said bitterly.

The party favors included cocaine. He'd done coke a few times—enough to know he didn't particularly care for it. Give him some tequila shooters any day. But Kate had never tried the stuff until that night. And she liked it. A lot.

He came back to sag down in the chair. "I didn't realize what was happening at first. They laid off a couple of guys at work and expected the rest of us to take up the slack. I was out of town all the time. Kate went through everything, our savings, the investments. One day I came home from a trip and found she'd sold Goldy and the money was already gone. She sold anything she could get a dollar for and stuffed it all up her nose. She didn't close any deals. Her income dried up. We had to take out a second mortgage just to stay afloat."

Patterns, I thought, remembering the other day when I stood in Robb's kitchen.

I said, "Any chance Lee Gersky was supplying the cocaine?"

Robb was too wrapped up in the anguish of his story to express any surprise at the accuracy of my guess.

"That sneaky bastard. I didn't catch on at first. Tamra was always coming over. She was horse crazy, and Ben wouldn't buy her one. He used to talk about the droppings, like a horse was a dog who'd be coming into the house and messing up the floors."

"So Tamra would come over and ride Goldy. Kate didn't mind. Sometimes she was too busy to take care of the animal. Tamra helped with that too. And after Tamra started junior college and met Gersky, he'd tag along.

"I can't imagine what Tamra sees in the guy," Robb said. "I think she goes out with him mostly because it bugs her dad so much. And it wasn't like I knew for sure that Lee was getting the stuff for Kate. I asked her once, straight out, but she started a fight and never did tell me. She always did that, whenever I tried to talk to her about her problem."

"If you were right about Gersky," I said, "do you think Tamra knew he was dealing? Was she in on it?"

"Ah, Christ, I don't know. I told you, I'm not sure about any of it. I mean, I couldn't prove it. It was a feeling. I just *knew*."

Although Robb had no proof, somehow I thought he was right about Gersky. And if Gersky was supplying Kate with coke, it was damn likely Tamra knew about it. That meant I could add another scenario to my growing list: Kate's into Gersky for a lot of money; he cuts her off; she threatens to turn him in. And where was Tamra in all this? Witness? Or accessory to murder?

I felt as sick as Robb looked. And Robb picked up on it.

"Gersky," he said. "My God, he killed Kate, didn't he? And then he ran off with Tamra."

"It's a possibility," I said. "But we can't pin everything on that one theory. Did Kate make any new friends? Did she start hanging out someplace different?"

"I don't know. We didn't talk anymore. I felt she was keeping secrets, but I was getting so paranoid, maybe that was just my imagination."

"Well, think about it. Make a list, everybody she knew. Do you have a pool man? A gardening service?"

"We did at one time," he said. "We had a lot of things. But not anymore."

Well, I had figured as much. I told him I'd like a look at his records. Maybe I would find a check she wrote or a credit card receipt that should help.

"As soon as I get out of here," he said.

If he did. Of course, I didn't say that. I said, "I'll stop by in the morning to pick up those lists."

He promised he'd do everything I had asked, already looking forlorn as I buzzed the guard.

"Can I call somebody for you?" I asked. "Kate's sister, or your family?"

"No, I'd rather Rose didn't hear this from a stranger. And I don't have anybody except my parents. They're down in Florida. My dad has Alzheimer's. My mom has enough to worry about. I couldn't tell her the truth about Kate's death. I said it was an accident. I just keep thinking," he said. "I should have *done* something, you know? Locked Kate up in her room. Dragged her off to a clinic. People do things like that, don't they?"

The guard came in. Young, a recruit, I guessed, putting in his jail-duty time. I could see Robb drawing inward, steeling himself for the return to a cell.

"Listen," I said, "I'm going to do everything I can, so you just hold on. Take it a day at a time. And about Kate. Intervention might have worked, but there's a very good chance it wouldn't have done any good at all, not if she wasn't ready to accept help."

"At least I could've tried," he said. "How am I going to live with myself knowing I didn't try?"

CALL ME A SUCKER but I left that room convinced that Robb was innocent. And more certain than ever that I had to find Tamra and Lee Gersky.

Danny was still at the office checking hotels, but so far no luck. I sat behind my desk, staring down at my notes, considering my options. High on the list was the need for a talk with Kevin Ross, Gersky's old roommate, and, if I had to, a visit to Gersky's other buddies across the way. I found Kevin's number and got him just as he was leaving his apartment.

"I'm on my way to work," he said.

A security job at a construction site, part-time. He hadn't been scheduled, but somebody was sick and he had to fill in.

"Maybe I can meet you there," I said.

"Oh no, I'd be fired," he said. "What do you want to talk to me for? I told you, ask Randy and those guys about Lee."

"I did, but so far they're not telling me anything. This is very important. Tomorrow, as soon as you can, okay? Let me buy you breakfast."

"I don't eat breakfast. Anyway, I have an early class and then work. I'll be home around eight P.M. Listen, I gotta go."

"All right. Eight o'clock."

After I hung up, I sat there, wondering what else I could do tonight. It was getting late, way too late to start canvassing the cul-de-sac in Nellie Gail. Anyway, I wanted to do that during the day when the hired help was around. I thought briefly about asking my old pal Gary to share his notes, then reconsidered the idea. Gary was the *policía* and that cut both ways. Out of fear, some of these people might tell him things; others, however, would clam up. So it was important that I conduct my own interviews.

Of course, I could go down to Hilltop Apartments tonight, down to 19D. Have a brew and swap innuendoes with Randy and the boys. Since my chances of getting some straight answers from these weasels was somewhere between slim and no way in hell, I decided I wasn't up to the hassle. I wouldn't discount the possibility completely, but I would talk to Kevin first.

Another long shot, but it couldn't hurt to let the apartment manager, Jerry Reeser, know I was still looking for Gersky. Was there an answering machine at the office? There was. I left a brief message, saying I would be in touch. After that I told Danny to go home. It had been a long day, and I wanted to make an early start tomorrow. How would he like to take a break from calling hotels and help me do the interviews down in Nellie Gail? Love to, he said and headed out to get his bike.

"Wait for me in the parking lot," I called after him. "I'll take you home."

It would be easy enough to put his bike in the back of the van. Anyway, I worry about him out on the streets this time of night. I was almost out the door myself when the phone rang.

"Hello," Erik said. "I wondered if I'd find you there."

"Hi."

My breath seemed to be hung up in my throat. Well, it's not fair, catching me by surprise like that.

"Bad habit," Erik said, "working on Sunday night."

"What? Oh—I was just leaving. Is the benefit over already?"

"No. It wasn't much fun alone. I left early. New case?"

"Sort of. If you called about dinner this week, I'm going to be pretty busy."

"That's not why I called."

"It isn't?"

"No. I just thought it would be nice to hear your voice, that's all. I won't keep you. Go on home. Get some rest."

"Oh. Well—good night, then."

"Good night, Delilah. Sweet dreams."

Hooboy.

The man had no idea.

TWELVE

I GOT UP EARLY, had my morning walk, and ate a hearty breakfast at Mom's to fortify myself against a trip back to the jail. Several other early morning visitors sat in the holding room, waiting to be called. I recognized one of them.

It was Matthew Scott, looking rumpled and tired, his tie loosened, his hair too long and curling around his collar. A battered briefcase sat on the floor at his feet. I hadn't exactly been avoiding Matt—impossible anyway since he was on the staff of the public defender's office—but the encounters were always awkward.

Naturally, one of the few empty chairs was right next to him.

We had been lovers for about six months, the affair already winding down when Matt put an end to it. This happened in the hospital right after the bombing when he told me any fool could see my feelings for Erik Lundstrom were deeper than I cared to admit.

"Hello, Delilah," he said as I came over and sat beside him.

"Hi. How have you been?"

"Okay." He gave me a wry smile. "Better anyway."

"That's good."

I could feel my lips freezing into one of those phony smiles you wear when you don't know what to say.

The thing is, while I discovered I was not in love with Matt, I like him a lot. He had been good for me, the first stable relationship I'd had since Jack died. A warm, comfortable man, decent and kind.

I leaned close to him and lowered my voice. "What do you think? Is it possible we could have a regular conversation one of these days?"

"It would be nice," he said.

The guard called Matt's name. Matt reached for his briefcase and got up.

"Call me?" I asked.

"I think I will. Sometime soon."

NO PRIVATE ROOM for Robb and me today. We met in the regular area, with other prisoners, and their visitors a few feet away. Robb's eyes were red-rimmed, and his hands shook as he handed a guard the lists he'd written to pass along to me.

"Nobody'll tell me anything about the arraignment," he said. "I haven't heard from Leah yet."

"It's early," I said. "She'll be here."

If he didn't make bail, Leah would have to arrange it so I could get into his house for his financial records and the telephone bills. I didn't have the heart to mention this to him just then. Something about the guy brought out the mother hen in me. And I hated to leave him there, but all I could do was say a few more soothing words before I headed over to Irvine to pick up Danny.

Danny insisted on bringing along his bike—in case I didn't have time to take him back, he said, dismissing the prospect of a twenty-mile ride with a shrug.

Notice I haven't detailed any of my thoughts about Erik during all this. I was trying very hard to put my feelings on hold and doing a fairly good job until I ran into Matt. After that I kept having these momentary lapses, which I devoutly hoped did not leave me staring dreamily into space just when I needed my wits about me.

Danny and I knocked on the first door in Nellie Gail about nine-thirty. A woman spoke to us over the intercom in accented English. A Vietnamese accent. She sounded frightened and was adamant that she couldn't talk to us. Danny took over and we were inside in two minutes. Was it a brilliant stroke to bring him along or what?

He was just as helpful with the Latino nanny two doors down—his Spanish was better than mine—and he charmed the only resident we found home, an older woman, Mrs. Maum, who lived on the other side of the Sannermans', all alone in the big house.

"My husband died shortly after we moved in," she said. "I just rattle around here. Ought to sell it, but I can't face moving."

She wished she could help, but she had been visiting her daughter in San Marcos for several days, including the day Kate died. She didn't know the Sannermans all that well, but they seemed like a nice young couple. Such a shock to hear about Kate and now Robb being arrested—it had to be a terrible mistake.

"It was some maniac who got off the freeway," she declared. "Like that one a few years back—the Night Stalker or whatever they called him, that Ramirez. We tried to put in gates and a guard here, you know, but the county wouldn't let us. Now look what's happened.''

Mrs. Maum did supply the name of a gardening service that took care of several houses in the cul-de-sac, although she didn't remember which days they worked.

She was our last stop except for the Wylie house. I'd noticed Elena arriving in the old Chevy Nova, although it had been impossible to keep up a constant surveillance, so I didn't know if Benjamin Wylie was home or not. I really didn't want a confrontation with the man, and Elena was sure to clam up if he was around.

From the car phone, I called Pacifico Lighting. Wylie's secretary said he was expected in at two o'clock. If he was leaving from home for the office, that meant I had a good half hour to kill before Elena would be alone.

Enough time for a run down to Der Wienerschnitzel on La Paz for a hot dog and a strategy session. Outside tables offered stunning heat and a choice of views: the crowded parking lot of a strip mall anchored by a Lucky supermarket or the freeway with an exit sign covered in fresh graffiti. Both came with fresh car exhaust. We opted for an inside booth preferring the smell of cooking franks, sauerkraut, and mustard with air refrigerated to the point that I changed my order from root beer to coffee.

''Why don't I track down the gardening service,'' Danny suggested as he picked up his chili dog.

''Huh?'' I said, a french fry poised halfway to my mouth, lost in one of those thirty-second flashbacks of Erik. ''Oh. Right. Good thinking.''

After talking to the gardeners, Danny would head on back to the office, run background checks on Randy Beaumont and Carlos Diego, then finish up with the hotels. I had Elena and Robb's lists to keep me busy. With luck, Robb would be home later and we'd have his financial records to plow through.

We polished off the fries, wiped smeary hands and faces, and went to take Danny's bike from the van. After he pedaled away, I drove back up to Nellie Gail. There I found a place under a tree on the street adjoining the cul-de-sac, where I waited an extra fifteen minutes just in case Wylie was late leaving his house. I saw no sign of him, not surprising since I pegged Wylie as the sort who was always on time.

Figuring the coast was clear, I left my shady spot and drove on back to the Wylie house. Just as I turned into the cul-de-sac I was seized by the feeling that I was doing all the wrong things. This happens at some point in every case and it's a miserable sensation. Worse, sometimes the intuition proves to be right.

As for my earlier description of an investigation—stumbling around, looking for that damned banana cream pie in the dark—well, sometimes you find that you are in the wrong room, and what you fall into is something left by a very large cow.

Elena answered the bell, recognized me, said, "Mr. Wylie is not at home," and started to close the door.

I leaned against it. "I didn't come to see Mr. Wylie, Elena. I want to talk to you. Please, I'm not here to get you in trouble, but I really need to ask you some questions about Tamra."

She shook her head, but she'd stopped pushing against me, and I thought the refusal was only a pro-

grammed response, because something was stirring in
her dark, secretive eyes.

"Mr. Wylie won't consider it," I said, "but I'm
afraid Tamra could be in a lot of trouble. If you know
anything, Elena, it might help her."

She stepped back and let me come in.

"We could sit outside," she said.

I followed her through the dim, dark house out to
the patio, the one I'd glimpsed from Wylie's study. A
breeze rippled the pool. It was warm, but not uncomfortable. A hot-pink mandevilla vine climbed up a
trellis in one corner, spilling large leaves and big,
trumpet-shaped flowers and shading a table. White
and yellow daisies rioted in huge clay pots. Looking in
through the tinted windows, the study seemed as remote as a polar ice floe.

"He never comes out here," Elena said, following
my gaze. "It is beautiful, no?"

"Very."

"Please." She gestured to a chair at the table. "I
have made a drink with lemons. You would like this?"

"Yes, thank you," I said, anxious to talk before
Wylie returned but not about to turn down the friendly
overture.

I sat down and waited. From here I could see the
Sannermans' barn and the line of oleanders that
marked the dividing line between the two properties.
A high wall blocked the view of the yard, however.
Kate's body had lain on the far side of the yard, well
away from here. Still, if the wind had been right,
surely the stench would have been noticeable.

Elena returned with a pitcher of lemonade and two
glasses on a tray.

"I give my notice today," Elena said, pouring me a drink.

"You're quitting?"

"I have another job. A nice lady. She lets me bring my daughter." Elena sat down and picked up her glass. "Rosa is only two years old. It is very hard leaving her every day."

"That's good," I said. "I'm happy for you."

We sipped our drinks. The lemonade was very sweet and icy cold. I don't have any great theories about getting people to talk. But I have learned one thing: technique plays only a small role in conducting a successful interview. Negative ions, the moon in the right house—it beats me, but there does seem to be a moment of cooperation, a window that will slam shut as quickly as it opens. When this happens, it's best to listen and say as little as possible.

"Was Lee Gersky here when Tamra left?" I asked just to get the ball rolling.

"Not then, but before. Then there was a very big fight between Tamra and her father."

I felt an exultant rush. I'd been right about Gersky and right to believe that Wylie had been keeping something else from me. That should teach me to trust my instincts.

"I have a son," Elena said. "Gilberto is seven. Now with Rosa and always working I see he does very many bad things that must be punished. And then I see this is because I never say good things to him, *comprende?* Tamra is the same. Her father never pays attention unless the music is too loud or she is coming home late. I think if she cannot get him to notice the good thing then she always does the bad.

"This Lee Gersky—" She shook her head and there was no doubt of her opinion of him. "Mr. Wylie says Tamra must not see him anymore. He will take away the money he give her each month. I don't *want* to hear these things," she added, a little defensively, "but it is impossible not to hear."

"Of course."

"That day—Tamra brings Lee here while Mr. Wylie is at the office. They go swimming. And then they go to Tamra's room. When Mr Wylie comes home, he finds them there. There is much yelling and bad words."

The way Elena told it, she went into the laundry room to start a load of clothes, but the shouting could still be heard. Finally, when things quieted down, she came out into the kitchen. A few minutes later, Tamra rushed in, carrying a suitcase, asking for a sweatshirt that was in the wash. Wylie heard and came to find her, picking up his harangue where he had left off. At that point Tamra grabbed her suitcase and marched out of the house with her father in her wake.

"The front door was open," Elena said. "So I went to see. She got into the car and drove away."

"With Gersky?"

"No. Alone. I think he left before, after Mr. Wylie comes home and finds them."

"But you didn't see him go?"

She shook her head, looking beyond me at the pool, and rolling the rim of the cold glass against her lower lip for several seconds before she said, "I did not see him, but he must come out here. They leave towels and clothes when they go inside. I find Tamra's things, but the others—gone." She shrugged. "Maybe he takes them quickly and runs away."

Or maybe he goes next door where Kate is sunning herself. There was no direct access through the wall, but he could have climbed the chain link fence that ran between the properties to enclose the Sannermans' pasture and come in through the gate. Or he could have simply gone back inside, out the front door, and walked on over to Kate's.

He arrives, already in a rage, to find Kate—what? Wired on cocaine? Strung out because she hasn't had a fix? Could an argument between them have flared so quickly and violently into murder?

Up in an L.A. ghetto recently a grocery store owner shot a young girl to death over a can of orange juice; the incident was picked up by a surveillance camera, the videotaped segment short enough to be a favorite news bite for the TV channels.

Yes, it was possible.

I wondered if Benjamin Wylie had been jolted by this possibility and had, just as quickly, shoved the thought away. Well, he had to deny it. If Gersky had struck Kate in the face that day with a hammer, the scene in Wylie's house had been the catalyst. Not only that, Kate acted, in part, as a surrogate, taking the blow Gersky must have wanted to deal to Wylie.

"Does telling this help Tamra?" Elena asked.

"I hope so," I said. "You did the right thing, Elena."

"I have told you one lie. The first day you come here, about Tamra's room. I made the bed with fresh sheets. Mr. Wylie said to do this."

Talk about right in character. Whisking away the evidence of his daughter's roll in the hay with Gersky and then pretending it never happened—that sounded like Wylie, all right.

"Elena, do you come out here often?" I asked.

She understood the question. "Only when Mr. Wylie is away, and he stays home after Tamra left until you find Mrs. Sannerman. That morning when I come to work, I smell something, but I never think—" She shivered in the warm breeze. "I will be happy to work someplace else."

"Did you see Robb Sannerman the day Tamra left?"

"The police ask me this. I did not see him."

She stood up, put the glasses back on the tray, and pushed her chair in place under the table, signaling an end to our talk, the tenuous connection broken between us.

"Did you know Mrs. Sannerman at all?" I asked quickly, hoping to reestablish the rapport, but she shook her head, picked up the tray, and headed inside, leaving me to trail behind.

We were in the kitchen when we heard the distant sound of a car door slamming. Elena tensed, and the tray slid onto the counter with a little crash.

"I'll go," I said, "I don't want to get you in trouble. Thanks again," and prepared to beat a hasty retreat.

Too late.

Benjamin Wylie came in from the garage through a connecting door. There was nothing to do but stand my ground and face him.

THIRTEEN

WYLIE STOPPED and stood there, tie loosened, suit coat over one arm, briefcase in hand. He looked at Elena and me, instantly jumping to conclusions—in this case the right ones.

"I've been waiting to talk to you," I said quickly. "I insisted. Actually I barged in."

He ignored my lie and turned to Elena. "I can't believe you'd go behind my back like this," he said, his tone injured and his face suffused with rage. "Get your things and leave—right now."

Elena lifted her chin, a glint of defiance in her dark eyes. "First you will pay me the money you owe me and then I will be happy to go."

He didn't like it, but he dug out a money clip, peeled off some bills, and thrust them at her. Then it was my turn.

"Damn you," he said. "You're determined to drag my daughter into that sorry mess next door, aren't you?"

"I'm trying to sort out the truth. That includes finding out if Tamra's involved."

He dropped his briefcase with a loud thump, threw his coat on top of it, and glared at me. Elena slipped out the door without a backward glance. I didn't blame her a bit.

"Don't you get it?" Wylie demanded. "I fired you. You have no right to keep sticking your nose in my business."

"I'm working for Robb Sannerman. That gives me the right."

He snorted. "If Robb ever expects to clear his name, the first thing he'd better do is find another detective."

"Look," I said, my patience rapidly running out, "whether you choose to believe it or not, I'm trying to help Tamra. I know what happened the day she disappeared; I know Lee Gersky was here. I think there's a good possibility he left in a rage, went next door, and got into a violent argument with Kate. I also think that even though you didn't see him waiting for Tamra, he hooked up with her shortly afterward, and that your daughter is holed up somewhere with a murderer."

"Oh, *Jesus*—" He shook his head in disbelief. "You've got it all figured out, haven't you? Well, you're dead wrong. That son of a bitch Gersky? He wasn't mad; hell, he was *bored*. You know what he said? 'Hey, babe, this is a drag. I'm outta here.' He didn't even have the decency to stick up for Tamra. He just took off. After the way he acted, Tamra'll never have anything else to do with him."

His story shook me a little. Remove the part about Gersky storming out and it did change the scenario.

"So now you know what really went on," Wylie said. "I'm warning you: keep on connecting us to that sordid affair next door, and I'll sue your ass for slander. Now get out of my house."

I went, gladly, pausing only to say, "I hope you're right about Tamra. I really hope you're right."

Because I could think of another version: Gersky goes next door for comfort; Tamra's the one who's furious—at him, at her father, and maybe at Kate.

Had Wylie considered this alternative? If he had, he'd quickly brushed the thought aside. His nagging fear had never been for Tamra's safety, but that she and Gersky were off someplace screwing like mink, and now he'd rationalized that possibility away too.

I wondered if he had hired another PI to look for Tamra, but somehow I doubted it.

Outside, in the van, I tried to reach Danny, but he wasn't back yet. I left a message that I was coming in. There was time to begin working on Robb's list, contacting Kate's friends, before my meeting with Kevin Ross. I might as well make the calls from the office.

Elena was two blocks away when I caught up with her.

"Get in," I said. "Where do you live?"

"I can take the bus."

"Suit yourself. But I'm heading north if you want a ride."

She hesitated, then came around the van, and climbed inside. Her address in Santa Ana wouldn't be more than a few blocks out of the way.

"I'm sorry about what happened," I said. "I'll make up for any money you lost this week."

"It is not necessary. If I tell my new lady, she will say come tomorrow. But, *gracias*." She hesitated, making up her mind, then said, "Have you talked to Tamra's mother? Sometimes Tamra goes there when she is angry with her father."

"I did. But I plan to speak to her again. Did you know Kate Sannerman at all?"

She shook her head. She also had very little to do with the other people who worked in the cul-de-sac. Mr. Wylie was home most of the time; anyway, he didn't like the idea.

We lapsed into companionable silence after that until I pulled up in front of a small, neatly kept house with a profusion of roses climbing over a rail fence. An older woman came out the door, carrying a little girl who straddled her hip. A young boy barreled around the house, followed by a girl who was slightly older, both yelling, "Mama! Mama!" They grabbed Elena as she stepped down from the van, the two talking at once. After a hug, she shooed them off and turned to say goodbye.

"They lose their manners for a while when I come home," she said.

"How many children do you have?"

"Five. I think Gilberto would be the last, but then Rosa came along." I'd never seen her smile before. It was a brief, bright illumination. "Life has many surprises, no?"

Considering recent events, I had to agree.

I BEAT DANNY back to the office by thirty minutes, time enough to open the mail while I listened to the messages on the machine. They included two sales pitches, a client complaining about an expense item on his bill, Jerry Reeser—the manager at Hilltop Apartments—returning my call, and then Sunni Hofer issuing an invitation to Erik and me for a party on Saturday night at the club, not specifying which club, but then we folks in the inner circle ought to know, oughtn't we?

Much as I disliked the idea, I couldn't dismiss it out of hand. I had a dozen investigative hooks in the water right now, but that didn't mean I'd catch anything. Come the weekend, the best thing I could do for my client might be to cozy up to the sheriff's department chief investigator.

And what would I say to Erik? I'd have to tell him the truth about the purpose of our date; he was too smart not to figure it out.

Just thinking about the whole thing made me want to go home, take a hot shower, and scrub myself with lots of soap. Like Scarlett I decided to worry about it tomorrow and called Jerry Reeser back instead.

"You said you might ask around about Lee Gersky. I was wondering if you came up with anything."

His call-waiting signal bleeped. He said, "Something new, as if I didn't have enough—hold on," and went off the line. He sounded harried and strained, a normal condition for him, I expected. When he returned, he said, "Sorry—you know I was thinking and—well, I did remember something about Gersky going to Las Vegas. I can't think where I heard it, though."

"Okay. Thanks. I'll check it out."

"It must be a real problem," he said, "looking for somebody like Gersky. You hear about people vanishing, and nobody can find them."

"It happens, but I have a pretty good success rate with missing persons."

"What's your secret?"

"Simple," I said. "I never give up."

His phone bleeped. I could hear his deep, steadying breath and could imagine his grip on the receiver, the twitch of muscle in his jaw.

"You'd better get that," I said. "I appreciate your help."

"If I think of anything else—"

Bleep.

"Right," I said. "Thanks again."

I hung up before I contributed another ten points to the guy's blood pressure.

The door in the outer office opened and closed. Danny sang out, "Don't shoot. It's only me."

His alert was not a bad idea considering my recent acquisition, although he really wasn't in a whole lot of danger since the Beretta was down in the van with the .38.

He had located the gardening service truck and had spoken to the crew. Their scheduled work day on the cul-de-sac was Tuesday, the day after Kate was killed. On Monday afternoon they were doing two yards on the street below. They did not pay attention to cars passing by, they told Danny, and had noticed no BMW driven by a man matching Robb's description.

One man said he remembered a car parked along the street at the bottom of the hill below the Sannermans', but he did not remember the make or model, only that it was not new and looked out of place. He had thought perhaps it belonged to someone who worked as household staff in the area.

The good news part of the report was that if I couldn't find witnesses who placed Robb at the scene, neither could Gary. Danny and I were deciding what to do next when the phone rang. It was Leah Bennett, Robb's attorney.

"I just got back from the arraignment," Leah said.

Bail had been set at a million dollars. Given Robb's financial condition, that was way too high for him to come up with the ten percent a bail bondsman would require.

"How's Robb taking it?" I asked.

"Not good. Have you found anything at all?"

I gave her what I had, which wasn't much and sounded like even less as I talked. The county had released Robb's personal effects to her. She said she'd have somebody bring over the keys to his house to me tomorrow—or later today, if I'd be at the office for a while.

"Today," I said.

I could go by Robb's place after my interview with Kevin. Not being one for pep talks, Leah just said to give her an update in a day or so and hung up.

Danny got busy on the rest of the hotels, promising the backgrounds on Randy and Carlos when he finished. Meanwhile, I began calling the people Robb had listed as Kate's friends and acquaintances—mostly the latter, I noted, and the majority of these business-related.

First I tried the ones designated as friends. As usual, out of five calls I reached only one live person, a woman who said she was in the middle of making dinner, a dog barking and a baby crying in the background. She hadn't seen Kate in a year, not since the baby was born, sorry.

I moved on to the acquaintances with similar results. Danny ordered a pizza. I nibbled on a slice in between calls, but I had little appetite.

All I could think of was Robb, stuck in jail until his trial, and I had a daunting moment—hell, downright scary—when I realized he could be spending the rest of his life in prison unless I found out who killed his wife.

You could call this a temporary loss of confidence; still, with a man's freedom hanging in the balance, I had to ask myself if I was up to the job.

I hoped so.

All I could do was try.

FOURTEEN

THE SUN HAD JUST gone down when I arrived at Hilltop Apartments. The parking lot was full, so I circled around several times looking for a place to put the van. Just when I was ready to go park in the mall across the street and walk back in, a Tercel pulled out of a space close to the unit where Kevin Ross lived.

The blinds were drawn in 19C, a minimum of light leaking through, but 19D was ablaze. The door was open so there was plenty of illumination to see Randy and Carlos out on the balcony, leaning on the wooden rail. Even with the window in the van rolled up, I could hear the music—hell, I could feel it. The body panels pulsed with the bass throb.

I'd changed my clothes at the office, trading my hot-weather outfit for jeans, T-shirt, and sneakers. Ordinarily I'd wear the T-shirt tucked in, but tonight I wore it loose, and, with only a minimum of misgivings, I'd clipped the Beretta's cunning little holster to my waistband. The gun lay snuggled in the small of my back, a lump, but still a lot more comfortable than I'd expected.

Well, what the hell, I hadn't bought the damn thing to keep the .38 company in the glove box. And any lingering doubts about packing a firearm vanished when I saw Bix come to stand in the doorway of 19D, watching me with the other two as I left the van and walked over.

"Hey, babe," Randy called down as I started up the stairs. "Couldn't stay away, huh?"

"Hey, guys," I said, playing it cool and casual.

A loud crash in the apartment and then the gray tiger cat streaked out and bounded down the stairs, hissing at me as he passed.

"Whoa," Carlos said. "Pissed-off pussy."

"Hey," Randy said. "Be nice. Delilah's not mad."

At the top of the stairs, I was close enough to see the mean, bright shine of his eyes—pupils dilated by some controlled substance, I'd bet, and voted for cocaine. Carlos was giggling and saying something to Bix. The music was too loud to catch more than a couple of lewd words. I might yet come to appreciate Guns n' Roses.

"You sure picked a good night," Randy was saying. "You did come to party, didn't you, babe?"

"Not right now," I said. "Maybe I'll see you later."

"Awww," Randy said as I turned to knock on Kevin's door, "you're deserting us for *Kevie?* That's *painful,* man. That really hurts. Don't know if we can forgive you for that one, babe."

Kevin opened the door then, sparing me any more of his sparkling repartee.

"Jerks," Kevin muttered darkly as I came in.

He shut the door, which muffled the laughter and noise but didn't block it out entirely. I figured that would take at least a couple of feet of sound-deadening material. Even with a thrift store couch and tables and a couple of white resin patio chairs, Kevin's apartment looked like a design showroom compared to the one across the way. There was a minimum amount of clutter, less than my place has at times.

Kevin played host, inviting me to take a seat and bringing me a Coke. He did this with a certain reserve, and a touch of awkwardness that brought a little flush to his pale skin. Partly the male-female thing, I decided. And here I wasn't even wearing my jungle green outfit and my gypsy earrings.

Of course, I was much too old for him. About the same difference in age as there was between me and Erik, I suddenly realized.

I made guest noises and sat on the saggy couch. Kevin took one of the chairs. His red hair was all damp springy curls, and he smelled of soap and Brut. Dark green shorts revealed skinny white legs; a striped polo shirt bared freckled arms.

"You must want to find Lee pretty bad." He rubbed one palm on the side of his shorts and kept his gaze fixed on the glass in my hands. "What's he done?"

"I don't know that he's committed any crime," I said, "but I'm looking for him in connection with that murder up in Nellie Gail last week."

"You are?"

I had his attention now; he forgot to be shy.

"How's Lee mixed up in that?" Kevin asked.

"Maybe not at all. Maybe as a witness. His girlfriend, Tamra Wylie, lived next door to the woman who was killed, and Lee was at the Wylies' the day of the murder. Then he and Tamra took off, didn't tell anybody where they were going, and I'm having a devil of a time tracking them down. Do you know Tamra?"

At my direct question, he ducked his head and went back to avoiding my eyes. "Not really. I met her a few times, and I see her around school. Saddleback," he said, tilting his head in a gesture that indicated the direction of the community college campus which sprawled behind the apartment complex. "I never could understand why she went out with Lee. Girls like guys like him, I guess. Maybe they like being treated like dirt."

"Some might," I said. "Not all of us, take my word. After Lee moved out, did he bring Tamra around next door?"

He thought about it. "I don't think so. Maybe she drew the line somewhere."

"Not a wholesome bunch," I agreed.

"I just try to stay out of their way," Kevin said, adding quickly, "there's not much else I can do. I don't take a lot of crap off people, but I'm not crazy. The problem is they're always around, you know?"

"Do any of them work?"

"Like a regular job? Off and on."

"But they haven't been evicted, so they must pay the rent. And they sure do have a world-class stereo system." The continuous low-cycle rock beat vibrated through the walls. "I've had a few neighbors like that, blasting away. Okay I guess, if you like the stuff they play."

"You don't, do you?" he asked.

I understand from the younger set that this is one of the most important questions to be settled between two people these days. Well, I knew what Erik liked: classical, one more of those basic differences between us.

I assured Kevin heavy metal was not my kind of music, relieved when he didn't ask for specifics. If he hated Dire Straits, our growing rapport would probably be over.

"So where do your neighbors get their money?" I asked.

"There's a lot of money in dope," he said, then added defensively, "They don't make any secret of it. Randy stands right out there and talks on his portable phone. I told the police that I've heard him do it."

"You reported this to the police?"

"Yeah, sure. But all that stuff about cracking down on drugs in Orange County? I can tell you it's total shit." Growing indignant, he shed his self-consciousness. "I told them, like send somebody down here. Bug his phones. The cops ignored me. I call them later and tell them how these guys are always threatening me, but they just go, Threats aren't a crime; call us if you wind up in the hospital. I gave up after a while."

"What about the manager? Have you complained to him?"

"Oh sure. At first, Reeser got on them about the noise; he even came over, not that it did any good. I think he just got sick of me calling up all the time. When I told him about the drugs, he went, Yeah, yeah, brushing me off, and then later he goes, These are serious charges. I can't accuse somebody without proof. What I think—he's scared of them. A few weeks ago they were leaving bags of garbage out on the balcony. Too lazy to take the stuff down to the trash bins. One night I saw a rat run across out there. Reeser didn't do a damn thing until I finally called the health department."

The lack of response from Jerry Reeser surprised me. Reeser had seemed more than willing to help me.

Of course, maybe he only responded to women, or to situations where there was no possibility of bodily harm. Then again, maybe he heard complaints all day long and had learned to tune them out.

Full of angry energy, Kevin jumped up to go in the kitchen and put more ice in his drink. I shook my head to his offer for a refill.

"How about the rest of your neighbors?" I asked. "Aren't they complaining too?"

"They don't seem to care. Maybe they're afraid or maybe they get their dope from Randy."

"Sounds like a terrible situation," I said. "Why do you stay here?"

He sat back down and gave me a disbelieving look. "Are you kidding? The management company won't let me out of my lease. I think they know they'll never rent the place. I sure can't find anybody to take it over. I can't even find anybody to move in and share expenses. I'm shoveling out all this money for rent and utilities; I'm working two jobs and I can't save a dime. Any place I go will want a deposit or first and last month's rent. I'm trapped here."

I couldn't help thinking of the waiter, Josh, who had served lunch to Erik and me at the Harborside on Saturday and contrasting him to Kevin. They were about the same age, but Josh had radiated a confidence I suspected Kevin might never have, a self-assurance that comes from wealth—Daddy's bucks or a big fat trust fund. Easy to take chances; so what if you fail? Come to think of it, everybody who worked at the restaurant had struck me the same. Maybe the help was pre-screened to make sure they were well housed before they were hired.

"When's the lease up?" I asked.

"Two more months."

"There's got to be something you can do," I said.

"You think so?" There was a touch of forlorn hope in his voice.

"Let me think about it," I said. "I've been in a few rough spots myself. I know how it feels. Now, about Lee—is he dealing too?"

"Sure he is. Well—I mean, I never actually saw him like Randy, but I'll just bet he is."

"How long have you known him?"

"Lee? Not long. I met him at work. He seemed like an okay guy. I heard he got drunk once in a while, but I thought, Well, hey, everybody likes a few beers. But Lee gets mean when he drinks. And then Randy and Carlos moved in next door, and Lee started hanging out over there almost right away. Pretty soon he was ragging on me as bad as they were. I got fed up. My name's on the lease, and he'd only paid for a month. He owed me almost nine hundred dollars. I told him to leave. He had the nerve to want his half of the deposit back, can you believe that?"

Kevin didn't know any of Lee's other friends, wasn't even sure he had any. Lee never hung out much with the people from work, but Kevin would give me names, I could ask them myself. As for school, Lee only took an occasional class, telling Kevin this was strictly to meet chicks.

Just then the music stopped, creating an eerie feeling, a kind of hissing silence in the room. I hoped for Kevin's sake that some major component had burned out in 19D's stereo system, something that could only be sent via a slow boat from Japan.

"How about Lee's family?" I asked.

"He never said much; his folks split up a long time ago. I think his mother lives in Vegas."

"Would he go there?"

"I don't know. I doubt it. He hated her, said she kicked him out while he was still in high school."

Kevin was uncertain whether the mother still used Gersky for a last name. He dimly remembered she'd remarried, because Lee used to talk about how he hated her old man, too.

I'd run out of questions, and, forthcoming as Kevin had been, I wasn't sure I had gotten anything useful. Depressing, because now I was going to have to take Randy up on his invitation. The feel of the Beretta against my back was a little comfort, damned little.

"I'm sorry," Kevin said. "I wish I could help more."

"You did what you could. I appreciate that." My smile started a tide of pink rising up his neck and reddening his ears. I stood, saying, "You'll let me know if you remember anything else?"

"Oh sure." He jumped to his feet, almost upsetting the chair, and followed me over to the door. "And if you think of something—I mean like you said before—about my lease—"

"Don't worry. I'll be in touch."

He mumbled an awkward thanks and opened the door for me. I could see now why the music had stopped. Nineteen-D was dark and deserted-looking. Kevin said that Randy and his friends sometimes congregated at a Mexican restaurant—Rosita's—down the street.

"Maybe I ought to go with you," he said, although I sensed his manly show of protectiveness was mixed with reluctance.

I assured him I'd be fine. He had enough problems with Randy and his pals. I certainly didn't intend to be the cause of any more friction.

Standing in the doorway, watching me leave, he reminded me of Robb. A bit of a stretch, but the guy was trapped here, by circumstance if not by law. I'd meant what I said about helping him. I knew a lawyer who would make mincemeat of the management company. Now, if getting Robb out of jail was only so easy.

I waited for the traffic signal at the apartment exit, considering. A left turn would take me to Rosita's; go through the light and I'd be in the parking lot at Mission Mall. It was nine forty-five. The lot was empty except for a cluster of cars around the entrance that served a three-plex movie theater. No restaurants. I remembered a Coco's on Crown Valley Parkway. I wasn't all that familiar with the layout of the mall, but I was pretty sure I could take a short cut through the lot.

I realized I was procrastinating, but I really was hungry, having had no dinner except the slice of pizza I'd eaten at the office with Danny. Anyway, it would be hard enough to deal with Randy and his pals on an empty stomach, and damned if I'd eat with them.

When the light turned green, I went straight ahead into the parking lot, angling left to circle the buildings on an inner perimeter road, musing about Kevin's story concerning the drug dealing next door. It didn't surprise me, and come to think of it, the ongoing party over there would serve as a perfect cover for people coming and going, picking up a drug buy.

Around the south end of the mall complex, on the opposite side from the theater with its lights and people and cars, a sign warned of speed bumps ahead. I braked and just then the steering wheel began pulling right, that feel of a tire going quickly and unmistakably flat.

I parked in an end lot and got out to check, swearing under my breath and wondering if there was any way I could change it myself. God knows how long it would take for the Auto Club to come, and my stomach was making rumbling noises.

No doubt about it. The right front tire was so deflated, I'd soon be down on the rim.

Sodium vapor lamps cast a sickly yellow glow on the big, empty stretches of asphalt. Lots of businesses down below near the freeway and along Crown Valley, but here, up on a hill, the back of the mall was pretty isolated. Traffic rumbled on I-5, a distant rhythmic roar that reminded me of the rock music pounding through the walls of Kevin's apartment. If I was uneasy at all, well, I'm as prone as the next woman to an instinctive surge of apprehension in a situation like this.

I started back down the passenger side of the van, deciding to take out the jack and at least try to tackle the flat myself, aware of the sound of an engine first and that it was growing louder, separate from the freeway, a full-throated V-8 growl.

I glanced over. A big truck, an overgrown pickup with no lights, blasted down the perimeter road. Suddenly it veered into the parking area—trying to miss the speed bumps, I thought. And it would do that, all right.

Only one problem: huge as a locomotive, unswerving as destiny, the truck plunged straight at me.

FIFTEEN

EVERY NERVE IN MY BODY shrieked a warning. An agonizing delay, all those neural impulses connecting, before I could act. I lunged off to the left away from the van, the only way I could go, a jarring, skidding roll on the rough asphalt. Metal screeched as the truck clipped the right side of the van. Brakes squalled.

Lying there, stunned and breathless, my fear was mixed with fury along with a large dollop of indignation. If I wasn't swearing aloud, my mind was full of vivid epithets. Drunken asshole, for example.

The truck sat next to and slightly ahead of my van, engine rumbling, the exhaust pipes burbling out a smell like rotten eggs. Dark gray body, a cargo net replacing the tailgate, impossible to read the rear plate. Mud, maybe. And with the tailgate missing, nothing to hint at the make of the truck. Nobody got out. Just as I drew in a lungful of the sulfurous fumes and began scrambling up, the driver stomped on the throttle.

"Hey you, come back here!" I yelled.

I fumbled with the Beretta, unfamiliar with the safety, thumbing it up, entertaining some half-baked notion of shooting his tires out. I was mad enough to give it a try because damned if I'd let him get away.

Then, almost as if responding to my shout, the pickup heeled around in a tight turn. The engine roared. A split second of disbelief gave way to terror.

I bolted toward the van, fueled by a surge of pure adrenaline, instinctively heading for the only available cover. I just made it to the back bumper when the truck careened past, missing me by inches.

The powerful suction of its wake made me stumble. I banged into the van's bumper and almost fell before I regained my footing, all with alarms sounding in my head because the truck was braking, the rear end skidding around, getting ready to come at me again.

I knew I'd never make it into the van. And it was quite likely I wouldn't be able to throw myself clear a second time. I'd be squashed against the bumper or between the two vehicles.

The truck howled toward me. Sodium lights glinted off the windshield, so the driver was just a hulking shadow behind the tinted glass. I leveled the Beretta and fired twice.

My first bullet ricocheted off chrome with a metallic ping; the second starred the glass in radiating lines in front of the driver. I was already moving, trying to get clear of the van, shooting again as I ran with no idea whether I'd hit him this time, not sure if it mattered. The Beretta was designed to be used for in-close and personal situations, not as a defense against a couple of tons of Detroit iron.

But the pickup swerved away, swaying. Back on the perimeter road, it bounced hard over a speed bump with a loud ka-thunk. The driver fought for control, straightening the truck out and speeding away. Another bone-jarring wham-thump as he hit the next concrete barrier, and then he was gone, behind a parking structure and out of sight.

I limped over to the van, moving as fast as I could, afraid he'd turn around and come back for another try. No broken bones, or at least I didn't think so. There was a long scrape down my left arm, the abraded skin oozing blood, and my jeans were shredded on the right knee. The old description about feeling like one had been hit by a truck was too damned close to the truth this time.

In the van I dialed 911 on my cellular phone. If I gave the impression the driver of the pickup was a homicidal maniac all set to return and mow me down, well, I did think this was a distinct possibility.

I could see his windshield in my mind's eye, the bullet hole square in front of the steering wheel but high. I hoped I had plowed the driver a new part in his hair, but I thought there was a good chance I'd missed him. The hit rate for police officers in the field is only one out of four and that's with a larger weapon and a lot more practice.

My instincts urged me not to hang around and wait for the police, but my practical side shuddered at driving on the rim which meant I'd ruin a tire, and—okay, I admit it—now that the terror had subsided, my natural obstinacy took over.

Sitting there, a little trembly and shocky, I scanned both the area up around the parking structure and my rearview mirror, just in case the truck circled the mall and tried to sneak up on me from behind.

Although I never had a clear look, my impression was that the driver had been a man. At least three likely candidates came to mind. I was trying to do a mental inventory of the vehicles parked over in the Hilltop lot in front of Kevin's unit when I heard the wail of a siren and saw a patrol car coming. Just as the black and white slid to a stop beside me, a beige Toyota sedan with a light bar flashing barreled up. A security patrol—and where in hell had he been?

Taking no chances, the sheriff's deputy got out with his gun drawn. Well, I would have done the same. The crazy guy could've been in the van with me, or I could be the wacko for all the cop knew.

I followed his orders to keep my hands in sight and got out slow and easy just like he said. The security cop was out of his car, too, young and gangly in his tan uniform, moonlighting like Kevin Ross, I'd bet. I couldn't see for sure, so I didn't know if he had a weapon. I sincerely hoped not, much more nervous about that possibility than I was about the trained patrolman's unwavering pistol.

"There's a gun on the passenger seat," I said. "The carry permit's in my purse."

Once he'd checked that out, everybody relaxed and all our levels of adrenaline lowered a notch or two. When I vetoed the young security guard's suggestion of calling the paramedics, he dug an emergency medical kit out of his car and wanted to clean up my scraped arm. I said I'd do it myself and asked him to call the Auto Club for me.

The sting of antiseptic hurt like hell. Once the initial pain subsided and my eyes stopped watering, I told the cop what had happened, realizing how few details I had to offer.

He reported that there were traces of dark gray paint on the gouges in my van, but all I could tell him was that the truck was definitely American, maybe a Ford, although I didn't know for sure. I had never seen a plate number.

"Probably doped up," the cop said. "Or drunk. Maybe just a nut case."

"I don't think so." I told him I was working on a murder case for the defendant's attorney. "Somebody doesn't like the questions I'm asking. And there are some pretty unsavory types involved." I named Randy and his two best buddies and said they lived over in Hilltop Apartments.

He listened, looking more and more skeptical. "Did you ever see the truck over there?"

"No."

"And you said you couldn't identify the driver?"

"That's right, but the *truck* should be easy to spot right now. It's got a bullet hole in the windshield, and I wouldn't be surprised if the slug isn't somewhere inside the cab."

"Well, I'll check around over at Hilltop," he said, although clearly he didn't hold out much hope of finding the vehicle.

Just as clearly he thought I was way out of line to fire at the truck. Although he didn't discount the danger, the cop thought it much more likely the driver had been a stranger, horsing around, getting his deadly kicks at my expense.

"You could've killed the guy," he said severely.

I kept my mouth shut, because, of course, this was exactly what I'd hoped to do. I'd pulled the gun without hesitation and felt a kind of remorseless joy when I fired. The memory shook me a little, as did the knowledge that I'd do the same thing again.

His lecture on arms control was cut mercifully short when he got another call, an accident on the freeway. He left, siren wailing, just as the Auto Club mechanic arrived. Any investigation of the attempt on my life was going to be way down on the deputy's list of priorities.

Still feeling shaky, I sat in the security patrol Toyota to wait while the inarticulate young guard went to hover over the mechanic who was jacking up the van.

I consider myself a rational person who would much rather talk than fight. And while I've owned a gun for years, having a weapon and firing it are very different situations. Still, for all my qualms about buying the Beretta, tonight I had used it without a second thought. Self-defense or not, I wasn't altogether sure I liked myself just then.

In addition, I had to consider that the patrolman might be right, that nobody was out to deliberately run me over. Random acts of violence sprout like weeds in the well-tended lawns of suburbia these days. Carjackings, drive-by shootings—a kind of group craziness fueled by drugs and a basic breaking down of the social structure.

The mechanic had finished putting on the spare. He carried the flat tire around to the back of the van, the security guard at his heels, set the tire down, and called, "Ma'am? You wanta come over here?"

Under the bright beam of his flashlight, he showed me what had happened. The valve stem had been cut, sliced about half-way through at the base of the nipple. No accident, the mechanic assured me.

Doubts and logic be damned. I knew the saboteur was the driver of the truck and that he had tried to kill me.

BACK WHEN I bought the van, I had splurged on a real spare to replace the little doughnut tire that came as standard equipment and was designed strictly as a standby. This meant the van could be driven normally—at least until something else got wrecked.

So with a clean burst of anger sweeping away any lingering doubts and most of my common sense, I headed straight over to Hilltop Apartments because, although I might not know who damaged my tire, I did know where it was done.

Nineteen-D was still dark. I cruised around slowly, looking for the truck. A person of modest intelligence would have ditched the pickup, but nothing about the incident showed a whole lot of smart planning.

Stuck over in the deserted mall lot, I'd provided a perfect opportunity for a hit-and-run attack, but it was more likely that when the tire went flat I'd have been stranded along the street or the freeway. Would the guy still have opted for vehicular manslaughter? Or was there some other plan? Maybe he would have played the good Samaritan stopping to help, then used the knife to do a lot more damage than slashing my tire valve.

Considering my chief suspects, I thought it entirely possible that the original act of sabotage had nothing to do with the Sannerman case, that it came under the heading of simple harassment, the kind Kevin was subjected to, with no follow-up planned. But once I became such an easy target, well, hey, let the good times roll.

There were lots of trucks in the parking lot at the apartment complex and lots more down the street at Rosita's; the damn things are ubiquitous as palm trees in the county, even more plentiful than minivans. One Ford looked like the one I wanted to find except the windshield wasn't cracked. Not a broken window in any of them.

By then hunger gnawed at my stomach, and I'm sure my blood sugar was bottoming out. My friends have learned to tread softly when I'm in this condition. Nobody had warned Randy and Carlos.

They sat at a round table over in the corner of Rosita's with three other guys and a couple of scruffy young women who looked like they were right where they belonged.

Some head-banging music blasted from hidden speakers, not even remotely south-of-the-border, so I'm sure they all felt right at home. The decor was Tijuana done by Andy Warhol. Everything in pink and green, plenty of mirrors. On the walls neon traced outlines of cactus and sombreros. More neon strips on the ceiling. The place was about half full of people, several of them raucously drunk, and smelled of frying tortillas, chili peppers, and beer with just a trace of marijuana.

Besides Randy and Carlos, I recognized the roommate, the one they called Jam, but the rest were strangers. The table was littered with the remains of nachos and some gnawed Buffalo wings, baskets with broken bits of tortilla chips, salsa bowls that looked like they'd been licked clean, two pitchers that were down to beer dregs and foam, and an ashtray full of butts.

Carlos spotted me first. "Yo, mama. Look who's here."

Was Randy surprised to see me? I couldn't tell. He gave me a smirky grin and said, "Hey, babe, you decided to join us after all." He eyed the nasty scrape on my arm. "Oh, wow, I'm gonna have to revise my opinion of ole Kevie. The man may have possibilities after all."

He took some care with the words, just drunk enough to be impressed with himself.

"Yeah, big surprise." I grabbed a chair from the next table and sat down. The Beretta made a comforting lump against the chair back. "Let's talk, Randy. No bullshit. No games."

"Think you better watch your mouth," Carlos said. "Tell her, Randy. We don't like no *putas* comin' here and gettin' in our face."

There was a general mutter of agreement around the table. Randy raised a conciliatory hand. "No, now wait. Delilah's got something to say, I'm willing to listen. Carlos, Jam, you can stay."

He gestured for the others to leave the table. They did, with dark looks and much foul language, to congregate across the room. Several people were now watching what was going on. About the only ones who weren't interested were the couple snuggled up in a nearby booth, a blond woman and a man with his dark hair drawn back in a ponytail.

"Hey, barkeep," Randy yelled to a waiter. "A double tequila with a wedge for my lady friend here. And another pitcher of Bud." Then, to me, "Okay, shoot."

"Interesting choice of words," I said. "Too bad I missed tonight. Next time I won't."

Carlos stared at me, incredulous. "You took a shot at somebody?"

"Oh, whoa, *babe,*" Randy said. "Still waters. Wouldn't want you mad at me. Wait—" He narrowed his eyes, and I could swear the pupils closed vertically like a snake's. "Now I get it. You were mugged or something, and you think we were in on it. Like when was this? We've been sitting right here since nine o'clock. Hey, bro, how long we been in your wonderful establishment?" Randy called to the waiter who was bringing over the beer and tequila.

"Too long," the waiter said, arriving with the beverages. "Who's paying?"

I gave him a look that said he had to be kidding. Randy handed him a twenty saying, "Keep the change."

Unimpressed, the waiter left.

"See?" Randy said.

"You may have been here," I conceded, "but where's your pal Bix?"

"Oh, man." Randy shook his head sadly. "You really ought not to stereotype people, Delilah. Underneath that nasty exterior, Bix has the soul of a poet."

"Yeah? Where is he?"

Randy shrugged.

"Long Beach," Jam said. He studied his beer dreamily, pupils big as saucers. I realized the smell of marijuana was impregnated in his clothes.

"And was Bix driving a truck?" I asked him. "Something big, charcoal gray, a cargo net instead of a tailgate. Just blink once for yes, twice for no."

But Jam had made his sole contribution to the conversation.

"You way off, bitch," Carlos said. "Bix tools around in a 'Vette."

There was confirmation along with a murky gleam in Randy's eyes. He knew who the truck belonged to, all right.

"So it was Gersky," I said.

Randy looked like he might burst out laughing. "Haven't you heard, babe? Lee lost his license. Wouldn't be legal for him to drive."

"Pass along a message," I said. "Tell him I'm going to find him and I'm going to nail his ass. Yours, too, if I discover you were connected to what happened to me tonight."

"Promises, promises," Randy murmured.

"One thing you need to learn about me, Randy," I said. "I promise you something, you can count on it."

I thought about making a dramatic exit: throwing the tequila in his face, or maybe slugging the liquor down in grand old western B-movie fashion and hurling the glass through the mirror over the bar. I settled for that old classic: stalking out the door.

All of which made me feel a whole lot better.

At least until I got out to the parking lot.

Sitting in the van, feeling every scrape, bruise, and sore muscle, I thought about Robb and how I had just blown a major opportunity of obtaining information that might get him out of jail.

Something else: I'd all but waved my PI ticket under Randy's nose, and he hadn't responded. Maybe he'd been too drunk to notice. Still, I wondered.

SIXTEEN

JUST DOWN THE STREET at the freeway entrance, I found a twenty-four-hour gas station with a convenience mart. There I wolfed a stale ham sandwich and washed down some Motrin with coffee that had been stewing so long it tasted a lot like battery acid. Rounding out this nutritious meal, I bought a package of Twinkies and ate those too.

Nothing like a blast of anger followed by caffeine and sugar to clear the old head and stimulate the thinking process. And what I thought as I finished up the killer coffee and went back out to the van was that drugs had left a trail through this case like a slimy snail track—Kate to Gersky to Randy and his pals.

And where were the cops in all this?

According to Kevin Ross, there was blatant dealing going on from apartment 19D. I knew for sure Kevin had called the police several times. Maybe other witnesses had too. Where there are little fish there are bigger ones, so why weren't the cops following up the food chain?

Then again, maybe they were.

I DROVE INTO the Hilltop Apartments complex just before midnight. Nineteen-D was still dark, but Kevin's lights were on. I passed up a couple of parking slots open out front, selecting a place several units away. After locking up the van, I pocketed the keys and walked back to Kevin's unit.

The streets in south county might be quiet, but things were still jumping in the complex. Cars were coming and going, contributing the noise from engines and car stereos to the sounds drifting from open windows: music, people talking, snippets of canned laughter from television sitcoms.

I shivered in a damp and chill breeze. High thin fog filtered the light from a lemon-slice moon. Ocean air was moving in, promising an end to the heat. I went quickly up the stairs and knocked on Kevin's door. A delay, and then the door opened a crack. I got a whiff of pizza and saw the glow of the TV—*Casablanca,* one of those films you know so well every frame is instantly recognizable. One look and I knew Claude Rains was about to order a roundup of the usual suspects.

"Ms. West?" Kevin said, astonished to find me there.

"Can I come in?"

"Sure. Of course."

I slipped inside.

"I was just finishing a paper," Kevin said, hurrying over to turn off the TV, make an untidy pile from the books spread on the couch, and shove aside a small, wheeled cart that held an electric portable typewriter. Then he picked up a plate from the floor, stopping to stare at me on his way to the kitchen, taking in the scrape on my arm and my torn jeans.

"Jesus, what happened? Are you all right?"

I glanced down at my arm. The abrasion was crusting over nicely but it still looked ugly and hurt like hell.

"Well, I'll have to admit I've felt better."

"Do you need a doctor? I could take you over to the emergency room at the hospital."

"Thanks, no."

He took his plate on out to the kitchen and put it in the dishwasher. "It was Randy and those guys, wasn't it?" he asked as he crumpled up a frozen pizza box and stuffed it in the trash. "I knew I should've gone with you. What did they do?"

I explained briefly about my encounter in the mall lot. "I went down to Rosita's and found most of them. And it looked like they'd been there awhile. Do any of them own a big truck?" I described the one that tried to run me down.

"I don't think so."

I asked, "What did Gersky drive—before he lost his license?"

"An old Z. You think it was Lee?"

"It's a possibility." Anything was possible. The truck could have been stolen, for example. "Listen, Kevin, I need to ask you a favor, and I don't have a lot of time to explain."

"What is it?"

"I want to keep an eye on what's going on outside for a while. Check out who's coming and going." Both the living room and bedroom had windows that could serve as surveillance points. I told him I could watch from the other room for now. When he was ready to go to bed, I'd move out here. "Is that okay?"

"Well, sure. I don't care. Hey, you know, I have a pair of binoculars. Want to borrow them?" he asked, eager to be a part of the action.

I didn't want to tell him that a stakeout is usually about as exciting as watching cars rust. I took the binoculars and thanked him. He carried a patio chair into the bedroom and fussed around positioning it and adjusting the blinds so I could see out but not be seen.

"Are you hungry?" he asked. "I have another pizza in the fridge, or I could make you a sandwich."

"Thanks, but I just ate."

I made a sweep around the nearby apartments with the field glasses and decided they were a good idea.

"You think you'll see the truck and get a look at the driver?"

"Something like that," I said. "You go finish your paper. I'll be fine in here."

He went reluctantly, and I tried to find a comfortable position beside the window in the dark bedroom. My right leg ached, and when I gingerly touched my shin below the tear in my jeans, I had to suppress a yelp of pain. I found it helped to prop my foot up on the window ledge—something about blood flow, I suspected.

This proved to be a temporary fix because pretty soon my ankle started aching. I thought longingly of the Jacuzzi at Ultimate Fitness. Rita would give me the key to the gym if I asked and if I could put up with her nagging me about taking better care of myself. It was hard to explain that I didn't plan these situations, that I did honestly try to avoid danger.

I remembered the uneasiness I'd experienced driving to Nellie Gail to see Wylie and then again when I'd stood in Tamra's room looking down at the hill behind the Sannerman house. In hindsight these were premonitions; at the time I thought I was just running scared.

One could argue, I suppose, that I not only attract trouble, I expect it. Well, I'd gone out and bought the Beretta, hadn't I? Was this an act of self-preservation? Or preparation for a self-fulfilling destiny?

Fortunately, the arrival of Randy and the gang saved me from any more probing of my subconscious.

The contingent had grown to three carloads. They all piled out and pounded up the stairs. As soon as the first guy was in the door of their apartment, the stereo went on. I wondered how Kevin ever managed to sleep.

"They're back," Kevin stage-whispered from the bedroom doorway, startling me. "Do you see anything?"

"Not yet. Do you want me to get out of your way so you can go to bed?"

"No, I was just checking." He stood there for a moment, then came over to stand beside me and stare down into the parking area. "You have to have a lot of patience to do this kind of work, don't you?"

"Yes, you do."

And sometimes it paid off. Another car pulled into an end slot, and a man and woman got out. The couple I'd seen making out in a booth down in Rosita's, the blond woman and the man with the ponytail. Maybe their romance had cooled considerably, but I'd be willing to bet there was another reason why they were headed inside without even holding hands, the woman ahead of the man and moving quickly.

They disappeared behind some bushes that screened the entrance of the next unit over, the one designated with the number 21. I took another look through the binoculars, trying to make it appear routine, and I must have succeeded because Kevin said he had to get back to work and left me alone.

A few seconds later I picked up the woman coming off the stairs and walking briskly along a second-floor walkway which served two apartments, a duplicate of the layout between Kevin and Randy. The man caught up as she knocked at what was probably 21D, although I couldn't make out the number. I got a glimpse of another man opening the door, big and burly, then the two went inside.

A happy little ménage à trois?

I didn't think so.

I waited another fifteen minutes, just to make sure nobody else interesting showed up. Kevin was hunched over the typewriter when I came out.

He looked up eagerly. "Did the truck come?"

"Afraid not. It was a long shot, anyway."

"You're not giving up?" He sounded disappointed.

"I think I'd better. I'm pretty stiff and sore." Well, this was certainly true. "I need to get home, maybe take a hot shower and get some rest."

A wonderful idea that would have to wait. Now if I could get out of here without drawing the attention of 19D and other interested parties. A small window in Kevin's kitchen looked out on the balcony. I went over and cracked the blind. Nobody was outside at the moment, but, as usual, the door to 19D stood wide open.

"You probably want to leave without Randy seeing you," Kevin said.

"Any chance of that?"

"In here."

He led me into the bathroom where there was a standard-size window, opened it, and took a flashlight off a shelf. The beam revealed some metal rungs set into the building a good two feet over.

"For getting to the roof, I guess. I go out this way once in a while," Kevin admitted, shamefaced. "Do you think you can reach it?"

"Oh yeah. This is perfect."

"Listen," he said, "I'll keep an eye out for the truck."

"All right, but if you spot it, don't do anything, don't talk to the driver, understand? Just call me."

Not that I thought he would recognize the pickup. By tomorrow, that windshield would be replaced and maybe, if the guy had any sense, the truck would have a new paint job.

I said a quick goodbye, promising to stay in touch. My purse was a problem. I put the strap over my head as well as my arm and then positioned the bag around on my back. Hoping it would stay there, I swung out the window.

My shoulder protested the stretch, and my knee wasn't too happy either, but I made a safe descent and ended up behind some hibiscus, healthy plants with nice, thick foliage. From there I plotted a course that would take me unobserved back to my van where, after a moment of apprehension, I took off the holster and returned it and the Beretta to the glove box to keep my .38 company.

Funny how quickly I felt naked without the gun.

I also scrounged up a hooded, zippered sweatshirt and put that on, not only gaining some warmth but also a degree of cover. Randy and Carlos were back out on the balcony saying a rowdy goodbye to somebody. There was even a possibility that Kevin might already be playing detective and watching for big trucks with shattered windshields.

Moving quickly and keeping my face turned away from all watchers, I went back to unit 21 and climbed the stairs, pausing for a moment to note how well placed the apartment was, right across from unit 19.

The burly man answered my knock. His bulky frame filled the partially opened door, and he positioned himself so that I couldn't see his right hand—and the gun I was sure he was holding.

A wary once-over and he said, "Yeah?"

"We need to talk."

"Look, lady, it's late. Whatever it is will have to wait. The wife and I are getting ready for bed."

"You mean the blonde who was smooching with the other cop down at Rosita's?"

A swift intake of breath. "Shit," he said and let me in.

SEVENTEEN

I WAS RIGHT ABOUT THE GUN. The cop stuck the Sig Sauer in the waistband of his trousers, then in a couple of practiced moves had me up against the wall and was patting me down. I'd expected the search, which was why I'd left the Beretta in the van.

"I'm Delilah West," I said. "A private investigator. My ID's in my purse."

The female half of the couple from Rosita's was out of the room; the male, the guy with the ponytail, sat on a sofa with his feet propped up on a coffee table, taking in the action with a dark, sly gaze and an amused grin. He was sipping a Dr Pepper and smoking a cigarette.

"We know who you are," he said. "That first day you came snooping around—we ran your plates. What did you do? Go out Ross's back window?"

I could hear a toilet flushing, and then the blond woman hurried down the hallway. She moved like a tiger that had been caged too long and looked as though she was in better shape than either of the men.

"Jesus," she said. "What's *she* doing here?"

Nice to be wanted.

The cop doing the search finished by running his hands down my legs. This was not the most comfortable thing for my bruises.

"All right," he said. "This better be good."

"Jesus Christ, Hollis, you shouldn't let her in here," the woman said, going over to peer out the window, ducking around a video camera set up on a tripod to have her look. "Three months of this—I swear, if she screws up our case—"

"It's all your fault, Trish," Ponytail said. "Nobody's going to buy our act until you get into it more, let those old hormones start working, get hot for my body." He grinned and drained his pop.

"In your dreams, Frank," Trish said.

"All right, can it," Hollis, the burly cop, said wearily, then glared at me. "I hope you had sense enough not to blow our cover."

"Give me a little credit," I said. "Do I just stand here and hold up the wall, or can I sit down?"

"Sit." He pointed to a straight-back chair.

The room had been set up for work, not comfort. There was a minimum of furniture, but, in addition to the video camera, there was a sophisticated microphone pointed toward 19D, and a television and VCR on a stand.

Hollis said to Trish, "Keep an eye out, will you?" Then he slumped down on the couch next to Frank, his weight mashing down the cushions. There were plum-covered shadows under his eyes, and he needed a shave. A shower and a clean shirt would have been a good idea, too.

Boredom, fatigue, and a slacking off on personal hygiene—symptoms of a prolonged stakeout. I knew them well.

"We're not going to dance around all night," Hollis said. "What do you want that's important enough to come busting in on a surveillance?"

"I take it you know I was here earlier this evening. Well, somebody tried to kill me right after I left." I told them about the truck and my close call over in the mall parking lot.

Frank flicked ashes into his empty pop can. "What did you do? Screw up a delivery? Skim a little off the top?"

"You're really good at this, aren't you?" When the sarcasm failed to wipe the smug look off his face, I said, "Get a clue. You know Gary Hofer? Head of the investigative unit?"

"I know who he is," Hollis said.

"Well, check with him. He'll vouch for me."

I might not have been so sure of Gary a couple of days ago. Thank goodness for chance encounters—not to mention Erik's brilliant idea of a cozy promenade up the marina boardwalk.

"I'm working on the Sannerman case," I said. "The woman who was killed up in Nellie Gail last week."

"Hey, I'm impressed," Frank drawled. "How come you're slumming down here with us drug enforcement types?"

"I'm hoping you saw the person who cut my tire."

"Astro van, right?" Hollis asked.

I nodded.

"I didn't notice anything. You guys?" The other two shook their heads, no.

I said, "How about videotape?"

"Where were you parked?"

"Just past the reserved spots."

"I'm pretty sure that's out of the field of view," Hollis said.

"Mind if I look?"

"Go ahead."

Trish moved aside to let me peer through the eye-piece. The frame included the landing outside 19C and 19D, the stairs, and the parking area right in front of the unit. The dark lot was amazingly clear, so I assumed there was some kind of image enhancement going on. The balcony was lit up like daylight, of course. Randy had gone outside, but Carlos was out there along with another guy, one I recognized from Rosita's.

"Well?" Hollis said.

"You're right. The van wouldn't have been visible from here, but I'd still like to see the tape."

Frank made a derisive sound and wagged his head.

"Evidence in an ongoing investigation?" Trish said. "No way."

"I don't know what good it would do you," Hollis said. "Not if you can't see your van."

"Look, it's not like I know who was in 19D," I said. "But they all left, right? So if I look at the tape, I'll know because I'll see who came out."

There was a glimmer of respect in Hollis's eyes. He considered, then went over to flip on the television and VCR.

"Hollis, Christ," Trish said.

Hollis ignored her and put in a tape. Some rewind-ing and then fast-forwarding located the right spot. The quality of the picture verified my guess that the camera was souped up.

There I was on the tape going up the stairs and the cat whizzing down, Randy and Carlos and Bix doing their thing, all in herky-jerky fast speed and no sound, which, at least, spared me a replay of their asinine humor.

A couple of guys wandered in; a few more left, including Bix. Then everybody else trooped out, dispersing into mostly unseen cars. No Lee Gersky. Nobody else I recognized. A few minutes later I exited Kevin's apartment.

Hollis shut off the tape. "Any help?"

"No, not at the moment, but thanks."

"You have an idea who it was?"

"You mean besides everybody in 19D?" I took a picture from my purse, the one of Gersky, Tamra, and Kate and indicated Gersky.

Hollis studied the photograph and said cautiously, "Looks familiar."

"Have you seen him around this past week?"

"I haven't, no."

"How about the other tapes you've made? Do you keep them?"

"Not here. They go into the department for evaluation."

He passed the photo on to Frank who gave it a cursory glance and said, "Nope."

Curiosity got the better of Trish who came over, took the photo, and stared down at it. "I've seen him a couple of times, but not lately."

"How about either of the women?"

"No."

She handed me the picture, bored with the whole thing, and went back to the window. Frank lit another cigarette and watched me, a merry little gleam in his eyes.

"Now what?" he said. "Pay attention, Trish. We might learn something here."

"What about a log?" I directed the question to Hollis. "I don't need to see it. Just look at the day Kate Sannerman died and tell me if any of the major players over there slipped the leash."

Hollis didn't like it. I was really pressing my luck. But, reluctantly, he consulted a notebook on the table. "That was—?"

"Last Monday. A week ago."

"Everybody except the small fry's accounted for." He closed the book. "That better be the end of your questions."

I was suddenly aware of just how tired I was. I was getting a headache from the smoke and my whole body throbbed. "Just one more. You're here because Kevin called the sheriff's office, aren't you? Did you ever think of letting him know he got some response?"

"That's two questions," Frank said, "but who's counting?"

"Couldn't risk it," Hollis said, looking uncomfortable.

"The manager knows about the operation," I guessed.

Of course. No wonder Kevin's complaints to Jerry Reeser suddenly fell on deaf ears. I had another disquieting thought. "You suggested that Reeser enforce the lease and keep Kevin here, didn't you? Sure. Why raise any flags? Keep everything status quo. What do you care how miserable the poor guy is."

"Kid's got a mouth on him," Frank said. "Brings most of it on himself."

"Maybe it's his way of keeping a little self-respect," I said, remembering just how much I'd hated dealing with guys like Frank when I was a cop.

"Well, you're not helping any," Frank said. "Randy Beaumont called the manager tonight, bugged him at home. Told him you were here again, harassing the tenants. Just think about what Randy is going to say after tonight at Rosita's, how mad he's going to be at Ross."

I turned on Hollis and demanded, "How far do you let it go? Kevin gets jumped, do you just sit up here and watch?"

"Come on," Hollis said. "We won't do that."

"*You* won't, maybe." I got up and headed for the door, pausing to say, "I'm telling you one thing, and you can pass it along to everybody working this stakeout. If those guys hurt Kevin Ross and you could have prevented it, I'm going to make sure the press has a field day and that Kevin has a damn good lawyer when he sues both the department and you personally."

"I told you you should never have let her in here," Trish said.

I WENT HOME, but not before Hollis delivered dire warnings about the consequences if I blew the operation, connections with the department or not.

Threatening Randy Beaumont was one thing. Threatening cops is something else, and this was the second time I'd done it. Any exhilaration I felt was short-lived. I had a feeling that letting off steam like this was not something I ought to over-indulge in.

Nobody followed me up the freeway; a tail would be easy to spot in the light traffic. Not that I expected anybody to be tracking me. As I had explained to Robb, most murderers are not brilliant in the planning department. They just make it up as they go along.

Still, my instincts were on automatic alert. I wished I thought the man who attacked me—Gersky, probably Gersky—would not make a second attempt, but I had the feeling he would.

No messages on my machine at home, so I assumed Danny had not made any breakthroughs. Only one message when I checked the machine at the office: Robb, calling from jail, sounding terrified and abandoned.

I never had picked up the telephone bills and financial records at his house, and I'd made damned little progress on the lists he'd given me. What did I have to report? I wasn't sure he would be cheered by hearing of my close call. As much as anything, though, he needed to be included and kept up to date. Sitting in jail, feeling cut off and helpless, would drive anybody crazy.

Exhausted as I was, I still took time to clean the Beretta, the act drummed into me years ago both by my father and the instructors at the Police Academy.

While I worked, I remembered one more thing to add to tomorrow's list: a chat with Jerry Reeser. He could have played dumb that first day in his office and on the phone today; he had reason to, knowing about the drug enforcement operation. But he hadn't.

Why was Randy calling him at home? Maybe Reeser was on cocaine, buying the stuff from Randy. He could have told Randy that I was a PI. Addicts are easy for cops to pressure, so this could explain Reeser's cooperating with the stakeout. It also meant Reeser might know Gersky better than he was admitting. The man seemed to be strung out and a little desperate. Figure out a way to give him a push and who knows what might turn up?

And Marilyn Wylie—Elena was right. I needed to talk to Tamra's mother. Marilyn had not been forthcoming on the phone. Face to face, maybe I could get her to open up.

What else?

Gary, to tell him what happened tonight and see if he would prod the necessary people in the department to look for the truck, the two of us being such good buddies and all.

I wondered some more about the car parked down the hill from the Sannermans' pasture, the one the gardeners told Danny about. Something I ought to check on. Then there were still Kate's friends to contact, and—

Enough.

To accomplish anything, I needed a few hours of sleep. I crawled into bed, but as soon as I closed my eyes I saw the truck bearing down on me, the driver dark and anonymous behind the opaque window. My heart drummed a little faster with remembered panic. I punched my pillow and debated about getting up for a sleeping pill.

In the distance, a helicopter beat the air, growing louder until it was overhead. The window lit up with the sweeping beam of a searchlight. Somewhere in the distance a siren wailed. This is not the best of neighborhoods, not the worst either, but violence happens with deadly regularity. It's no wonder the sale of handguns is skyrocketing. The whole world has bought itself a Beretta and stands armed and ready for the dark, anonymous truck bearing down, the burglar, the rapist.

It scared me to think about how I'd used my weapon with no compunction tonight. All I'd thought about was how badly I wanted to nail the bastard who was trying to kill me. A reaction spawned by society or strictly my own?

I didn't know, but the Beretta was on the floor under the bed and easy to reach. Even with all the bad dreams, I slept a whole lot better knowing it was there.

EIGHTEEN

NEXT MORNING I skipped the exercise and slept in until seven-thirty. I could barely drag myself into the bathroom, let alone walk three miles. Overnight a lot of muscles in my legs and shoulders had knotted up. Although a hot shower loosened some of them, it didn't do much for the bruises and scrapes.

I wasn't really hungry, but I had a bowl of corn flakes so I could take some Motrin. Nothing like ibuprofen for reducing swelling and cutting pain, a real miracle drug. Still, I seem to always be taking the stuff, at times prescribed by my doctor in huge amounts.

After reading some scare articles, I've begun to wonder what the medicine is doing to my stomach, not to mention my renal system. I settled for half my normal dosage, decided to hold off on coffee for now, maybe have it with Robb, and went to get dressed.

The scab had soaked off in the shower, leaving the wound on my arm raw again. A combination antibiotic and cortisone ointment helped a little. I debated about a bandage, decided the wound would heal faster uncovered. I dug out a cotton shirt with long, loose sleeves, an old Banana Republic favorite in a pale olive green washed to a comfortable softness. A pair of baggy, lightweight beige slacks would hide my leg, which was a colorful mélange of black, blue, and purple from knee to ankle. And, fortunately, the weather had changed, so I could cover up and save myself a lot of explanations.

Outside, the skies were a soft gray, a marine layer of clouds that ought to clear by midmorning, leaving the temperatures mild. Anybody can be a meteorological whiz in Southern California. The patterns are long-term and predictable. Which may explain why we get comedians doing the weather forecasts on TV what with all that extra airtime to work on their stand-up routines.

I wore the olive green shirt loose over a black tank top and clipped the Beretta's holster to the back waistband of my slacks, thinking *Jesus* a moment later when I realized what I'd done. After only one day of packing the damn thing, the action had become routine. Well, I certainly wasn't going out without it, not after what had happened to me the night before.

As a measure of my wariness I wore the gun while I went down to the van and during the drive over to the jail, and especially while I stopped for some take-out coffee on First Street. Plenty of carjackers around, even one crazy enough to want the van with the ugly dents on the right side panel. Of course, I'd probably be dead if I made any move toward the Beretta, but logic was not the governing force here. We are talking paranoia, pure and simple.

Reluctantly, I locked the small gun in the glove box before I went inside to see Robb. Jail was taking its toll fast. He was gaunt and exhausted with a brittle, breakable look and shuffled his feet as he walked over to see me.

"Did you find out anything?" He gripped the back of the chair on his side of the panel, using it for support and grounding, as though he'd fly off in a thousand pieces if not tethered.

"Robb, come on, sit down." I slipped into my chair, trying not to wince when I brushed my arm against the table. "Have some coffee."

The guard had the plastic-coated paper cup I'd brought there for Robb. Robb shook his head at the offer. "I can't keep anything down."

"Did you ask to see the doctor?"

He nodded. "He said it's nerves, that it happens all the time in here. He offered me a tranquilizer."

"You didn't take it," I said.

Tranked, he might have gotten a decent night's sleep and that obviously had not happened.

"This place—" A visible shudder went through his body. "Anything could happen. I want to see it coming, at least. That probably sounds crazy."

"No, it's understandable," I said. "When you're caught in a situation like this, you want to hold on to some kind of control. In a day or two, things will get better—not wonderful, I won't lie to you. But you'll learn to cope."

"I don't see how."

"A day at a time, an hour at a time."

"Well, maybe, if I just thought there would be some end to it."

He looked at me with a hopefulness that bordered on hunger. It was unsettling how quickly I'd become his lifeline, especially since I often felt like I was on choppy seas in a leaky boat, bailing furiously.

I took a breath and tried to sound optimistic. "I got verification yesterday that Lee Gersky was at the Wylie house the day Kate died."

"Then he could have killed her."

"Or he might know who did." I wasn't ready to explore the other possibilities with Robb.

"Are you any closer to finding him and Tamra?"

"I think so, but I can't give you anything concrete to back up the feeling." I really would have liked some coffee, but better not—the smell might make him queasy. "We're doing a methodical search and trying to cover every angle."

"Like what?"

He was starved for specifics, but I had to be careful. I could tell him I was sure I was getting close to Gersky, maybe to the person who killed Kate, because of the incident with the truck last night. Or that I felt Jerry Reeser hadn't told me everything he knew.

Either way I was pulling a string that would unravel the whole story of the police stakeout at Hilltop Apartments. Blow the stakeout and even friends and pseudo-friends in high places might not be able to save me from the wrath of the sheriff's department drug unit.

So I said, "Wylie's housekeeper, Elena—his ex-housekeeper now—seems to think Tamra confides in her mother. I didn't get much out of Marilyn Wylie on the phone, so I'm going to see her—today, if possible."

I told him Danny and I were continuing to canvass hotels and motels and to delve into Kate's personal life: the people on the lists he had given us and her spending habits. This must have sounded more encouraging to him than it did to me, because he brightened a little.

"You'll check back with me?" he asked. "I go a little crazy sitting here, not knowing what's going on. And Leah, I guess she's good at her job, I'm sure she is, but she has other clients. I get the feeling I could become a pest really quick."

I didn't tell him that I should have some other clients too, especially if I want to keep on paying the bills. What the hell, I couldn't back away now. The attack last night made the case personal.

I promised I'd be in touch as soon as I could, adding, "Just don't panic if you don't hear from me. Sometimes I can't break away, and I shouldn't, not if it's something that might help you."

"Okay. Delilah? Leah said if anybody could find something to help get me out of here it was you."

"Did she really?"

He smiled for the first time. "Well, not exactly. What she said was that you were stubborn as a mule and you never gave up."

"Damn straight," I said. "And don't you forget it."

BY THE TIME I ARRIVED at the office, the small lot out back was jammed. I double-parked and went inside, looking for Harry. I found him mopping the hallway in the front of the building, handed him the keys, and asked him to take the van and circle the block a few times. If the man could be trusted with a Lamborghini he should certainly be okay with my dinged-up vehicle.

Upstairs, Danny was already at work. I hadn't realized I was limping a little, but Danny noticed immediately.

"What's the matter with your leg?"

"Oh, gee, I guess I must have twisted my ankle this morning. It's nothing." No point worrying him, and no time for explanations. This did mean, however, that I would have to call both Gary and the insurance company from the car phone. "What's the status on the hotel search?"

The news was not good. Neither Tamra nor Gersky was registered, at least under their own name, in any motel, hotel, or bed and breakfast from San Francisco to San Diego or in any of the other counties near L.A.

I gave Danny Robb's list and asked him to take a shot at reaching Kate's friends and acquaintances and find out if she'd been in touch with any of them lately.

"Right," he said. "Then I'd better do those background checks on Randy Beaumont and Carlos Diego. I still didn't get to them."

"Just put that on hold," I said, since I now knew plenty about the two—although I couldn't tell Danny that without a lot of explanations.

"How come?" he asked.

"We can safely assume they're sleazes. Let's don't waste any time on them."

I would make a swing down to south county to pick up Robb's financial records, then maybe stop by to see Jerry Reeser. I would also track down Marilyn Wylie.

I thought about the other car again, the one the gardeners had noticed, but this was going to require more legwork than I had time for today, not to mention that I wasn't up to all that door-to-door stuff physically.

"Take care of your ankle," Danny called after me as I collected some phone numbers and addresses and headed out the door.

Going downstairs, I had a view of the back parking lot, of somebody pulling out and of Harry swinging the van into the vacated space, and then, seconds later, before I had walked—well, limped—down the last steps, I saw Erik's Lamborghini cruising in.

My head told me Erik's appearance was the last thing I needed this morning, but try to explain that to other treacherous parts of my body. Harry, of course, was delighted to see Erik, or at least to see his car. He rushed over to open the door for Erik just as I came outside.

"Mr. Lundstrom, say, it's great to see you again." The old guy was beaming.

"Good morning, Mr. Polk, how are you?"

Erik offered his hand, which Harry pumped warmly.

"I'm fine, just fine. Miz West couldn't find no parking, so I been out driving the van around for a while. Miz West, look who's here."

"Hi," I said, sparkling dialogue being my forte.

Erik looked so good a camera crew from some slick men's magazine ought to be arriving at any moment. He wore a blue-gray suit, perfectly tailored of course, a shirt in a muted pink color, and a tie that combined navy and a dark fuchsia in the most tasteful design possible.

When he looked over at me and said hello, I found myself grateful for overcast skies, which meant he wasn't wearing sunglasses. Well, I know it's pathetic, but that's what the man does to me. The most inane thoughts pop into my mind. While I was trying to come up with something as scintillating as my last bit of conversation, Harry let out a squawk.

"Oh, Jesus, Joseph and Mary," he wailed. "I didn't do it, Miz West. I swear I didn't."

He was staring, aghast, over at my van. The way it was parked, the long, fresh gouges on the side panel were fully exposed.

"Honest," Harry said, "I wasn't even driving more'n fifteen miles an hour."

"I know, Harry. Calm down. It happened yesterday in the parking lot at the mall."

"Did you see who did it?" Erik asked.

"No, afraid he took off."

This was absolutely true as far as it went, but Erik was looking at me like he knew there was more I wasn't telling.

"What are you doing here this time of the morning?" I asked, trying to distract him.

"I have a meeting in the county building at ten. I was hoping I could talk you into going for a late breakfast."

"Oh," I said. "I wish I could." Well, that certainly was true. "I'm really swamped."

"Coffee," he said. "Half an hour."

"Well..." By the time I left Robb, the take-out coffee had been cold and undrinkable, so I really needed an infusion of caffeine. "Okay, but it'll have to be quick."

I collected my keys from Harry and gave him a few more reassurances while Erik came around to open the

car door. He was just that much older and of an age
where these little courtesies were instilled in a man and
never mind feminist sensibilities. I got in, careful not
to bang my leg or my arm, wondering what it would
be like if I wasn't always keeping secrets.

He asked for a local coffee shop, and I suggested
Norm's. Harry waved as we drove off.

There's something particularly intimate about a
sports car. Maybe the small, enclosed space, that low-
slung seating—Jesus, face it, you're almost lying
down—or maybe the powerful throb of the engine.

Whatever.

The car was having an effect on me, until Erik
glanced over and said, "This guy who hit you—he
leave a note or anything?"

"No, just drove off."

"You don't seem particularly upset."

"Not now. Last night was a different story."

The Beretta, retrieved from my glove box as soon as
I left the jail, pressed into the small of my back, a
tangible reminder of just how different. I wondered
how Erik would feel about me if he had witnessed that
scene at the Mission Mall and knew what I was capable of doing.

At Norm's, bent on steering the conversation away
from last night's incident at the mall, I told him about
the call from Sunni Hofer and her invitation to a party
on Saturday night.

"We can go if you like," he said.

"You wouldn't mind—"

When I hesitated, he supplied, "Being used?" He
grinned. "Let's say I see it as a bargaining chip."

I could feel my cheeks getting warm. "Let me think about it. I'll let you know."

A refill on the coffee and a few more pleasant moments, then I was looking at my watch.

"I guess we'd better go," Erik said regretfully.

I'd been careful, exerting a lot of effort to walk normally and not favor my sore leg. Then we arrived back at his car, he opened the door, and I banged my arm against it. I let out a yelp and sat down—well, sort of *fell* down backward because of those damn low seats. I swore, too. The pain was pretty intense.

"What is it?" Erik asked.

"Nothing."

I guess I looked like a bird with an injured wing as I turned in the seat and tucked my feet inside the car.

"Don't give me nothing," Erik said. "You've hurt yourself."

"Let it alone, Erik. I'm fine."

He leaned down, glaring at me, those beautiful blues now about the temperature of an acetylene torch. "Listen, lady, remember a few months ago? I'm the one who heard over the car radio that your office had been bombed, who couldn't find out if you were alive or dead until I got to the hospital, and then I spent the next twenty-four hours sitting beside your bed to make sure you didn't stop breathing."

He slammed my door, came around, got in, and slammed his door, too. "Now what's going on?" he demanded.

"Okay, I was *in* the car when it was sideswiped. I bumped my arm. It's no big deal."

So far I'd been playing footsie with the truth. Now I was outright lying. Well, I had to. If he knew that somebody had tried to kill me the night before, I thought he might do something drastic: shanghai me and take me off to safety, call Charlie Colfax and hire a squadron of bodyguards.

God save me from overprotective men.

He was still eyeing me grimly, so I said, "Hey, I told you, it's nothing. Come on. Let's go. We both have a full schedule."

I was sure he didn't believe me, but he said nothing during the short drive back to my office, although the atmosphere in the car reminded me of thunderclouds gathering.

Harry must have been watching for us. He rushed out and opened my door two seconds after the car stopped moving. I was thanking Erik for the coffee and swinging around for a quick exit, when he grabbed my wrist. I think of Erik as a powerful man, a power that comes from wealth and influence. It was the first time I'd realized he was physically strong as well.

My resistance was immediate and instinctive. Our war of wills lasted for about three seconds while his expression went from primal masculine possessiveness to rueful apology.

He released me, put both hands back on the steering wheel, and said, "Delilah, you damn well better take care of yourself."

For once I didn't have a comeback, so I just got out. As soon as Harry shut the door, the Lamborghini roared off, leaving me to stand there and think that I ought to be feeling a lot more outrage and a lot less of a sudden urge to wave him back, jump into the car, and drive off with him.

Harry had heard Erik's last remark. "You in some kinda trouble, Miz West? Why don't I run up and get Danny? The two of us can come along—"

Lord.

I beat it out of there, but I still had the memory of one more worried male face to deal with.

NINETEEN

I WAS BARELY OUT of the parking lot when the car phone rang. "Where have you been?" Danny asked. "I called three or four times. I was afraid something had happened."

Harry had not yet hotfooted it upstairs to make a report, I suppose.

"I just stopped for coffee," I said. "What's up?"

"Gary Hofer wants to talk to you right away. I thought you'd want to know in case he's heard something about Tamra Wylie."

I promised I'd call Danny if I learned anything and hung up. The pain in my arm had eased a little, but it still wasn't a good idea to drive and talk on the phone at the same time. I turned down a side street and parked.

This was an area of small postwar bungalows, some of them maybe built by Erik's father, a family-type neighborhood that now had bars on the windows, chain link fences, and graffiti on any exposed surface.

While I dialed the sheriff's office, an old couple walked past with an elderly white poodle on a leash and eyed me with suspicion. I hoped Danny was right about why Gary had called me, but, unfortunately, he wasn't.

"That was a pretty dumb stunt you pulled last night," Gary said without much preamble.

"You mean almost getting myself killed?"

"Huh? Oh, the thing in the parking lot. No, I was talking about your busting in on a stakeout. The head of the drug unit was on the phone bending my ear first thing this morning."

"Oh, how nice," I said sweetly. "I knew you'd put in a good word for me. Thanks."

"Well, uh—"

I could just picture him squirming.

"I did what I could to calm him down," Gary said, "but the guy was pretty upset. I told you working for Sannerman was a bad idea. You could wind up in a lot of trouble."

"I'm already in trouble. Somebody sliced my tire and then tried to run me over."

Was there any possibility that Gary would push to have the truck found?

Fat chance.

"Yeah, well, you hang around with scum, what do you expect?" he said, verifying my pessimism.

"Gary, I don't think this happened simply because I was in the vicinity of some drug dealers."

"Let me guess. You're running around asking questions about Lee Gersky, so naturally that's why you got clipped."

"It's a logical assumption."

"Yeah. So was predicting the earth was flat. Stop trying to blow what happened out of proportion. You pissed some people off and they came after you. Simple. And if you keep sticking your nose where it doesn't belong, don't expect me to cover for you with the department."

The old Gary. I almost liked him better this way. However, I couldn't help saying, "Right. Got it. Oh, by the way, tell Sunni I'm sorry I didn't get back to her about the party."

Silence, then, "Sunni called you?"

"Yes. Erik and I discussed it this morning. We'd really like to come, but our schedules are so busy—can we let you know in a day or so?"

"Uh—sure. Yeah. You bet. Ah—Delilah, listen, sorry if I came down on you a little hard. I worry about you, you know?"

"I appreciate your concern," I said, trying to keep the sarcasm out of my voice. "What about the APB on Gersky and Tamra Wylie? Any word?"

"Nothing. You sure I can't talk you out of working for Sannerman?"

"Afraid not."

"Well, then, be careful, and stay away from Hilltop Apartments."

I could almost believe his concern was genuine after all until he added, "Don't forget to give us a call about the party."

"Oh, I won't. And, Gary, don't mention the incident down at the mall to Sunni, okay? No point in worrying her." Or giving her the opportunity to pass the information along to Erik.

"Right," Gary said. "I agree. See you Saturday."

Talk about your tangled webs.

Pretty soon I'd have to keep a chart showing what lies I'd told and who I'd told them to.

By now it was 10:15 and the sun had just broken through right on schedule. While I was stopped, I thought I might as well make a couple more phone calls. However, it was getting hot in the van, and the old couple with the poodle was back, pausing to stare before they unlocked a gate a house or two away and scurried inside. I'd bet the first thing they'd do was call the cops to report a dangerous-looking woman lurking outside.

I headed for the freeway.

I should have been reviewing strategy on the drive south. Instead, I was thinking about the male tendency to hover. Maybe it's instinctive, the old hunter-protector thing. Much as I had loved Jack, that side of our marriage had been a pain in the butt. Still, Jack may have been overprotective, but at least he was in the business and trusted my instincts enough to let me do my job.

Somebody else—okay, *Erik;* who the hell else was I brooding about?—Erik would worry constantly. And while I wanted a man in my life, was I really ready to put up with all the changes such a relationship would bring? Make a commitment and the guy would have a right to worry, a claim on me so I'd be answerable for my safety.

Jesus, listen to me.

Like I was actually considering having a relationship with the man. What had I told Rita? *It's never going to work.* Look at it objectively and guess what?

I was right.

GARY HAD WARNED me off Hilltop Apartments, so, naturally, that was my first stop. I even thought of going by to say hello to the guys on stakeout. But it's one thing to tweak the lion's tail, quite another to pull his whiskers.

I settled for the management office where blue and white pennants had been strung on lines running from the roof to the ground, and a sign offered move-in specials. Nothing about how the company made it impossible to leave if you got drug dealers for neighbors.

I hoped to catch Jerry Reeser before he left for lunch, but no such luck. Both Wendy Cole and the other woman—Maria Lucci—were at their desks. Reeser's glassed-in cubicle was empty. The office was in its usual state of chaos with both women on the phones and all the buttons lit up on the instruments, indicating people on hold.

I stood there, waiting. I heard Ms. Lucci say goodbye. Before she could take another caller, I said, "Hi. I'm looking for Jerry."

"Aren't we all?" she said sourly. The phone rang. She answered it with "HilltopApartmentspleasehold," and quickly reduced the caller to a blinking light. "Are you interested in seeing a rental unit? We have some nice two-bedrooms."

"No, it's personal," I said. "If you can give me an idea of how long he'll be, I'll come back."

She shot me a look that said any friend of Jerry's was definitely not a friend of hers.

"He never came in today. He *said* he had the flu, but he looked all right yesterday. I think he took the day off and went to the beach—and us with a promotion going on." The phone gave a reminding beep. She muttered, stabbed a button, barked, "YescanIhelpyou?" then turned away with her back to me while she talked, like she was dealing in state secrets.

I moved over to wait for Wendy to finish her call. When she did, I said, ''Hi, Wendy? Remember me? I came by the other day to see Jerry.''

This got me some vague recognition. Before she remembered too much, I added, ''I was supposed to meet Jerry here for lunch, but I understand he's sick.''

''Yeah, a bug or something.''

''Well, the thing is I've been running around all morning, so he couldn't call me, and I don't have his home number—I mean, I have it, but not with me. Could you give that to me? He's probably worried about missing our lunch date. Anyway, I'd like to make sure he doesn't need anything.''

''Well—we're really not supposed to—''

The damn phone rang again. She answered it. I picked up a Post-it pad and a pen off her desk and put them in front of her, mouthing *please,* hoping she'd hurry the hell up before Ms. Lucci cast her scowling glance on us.

Wendy finally, and with agonizing slowness, lifted some files to consult a list and scribbled a number. I grabbed the paper, framed a silent *thanks,* and hurried out.

Like Ms. Lucci I doubted that Reeser had the flu unless it was the blue variety. Not that I blamed the guy for escaping for a day. He not only had the pressure cooker of his job, there were also the cops, if my suspicions came anywhere near the mark. I just hoped he was home and not off unwinding someplace else.

But if he was there, he wasn't answering. When I dialed from the van, I got his machine—what else? I left a message saying that it was urgent I speak to him and left numbers for both the office and the car phone. Then I called Marilyn Wylie at work and was told that I'd just missed her.

The problem with my job, I mused as I left Hilltop, was that nobody was ever where they were supposed to be. Just nailing people down consumed big hunks of time. Of course, it was approaching the lunch hour, as my stomach reminded me. I drove across the street into the shopping mall, retracing my route of the night before, once again trying for Coco's.

There was nothing sinister at all about the lot in daylight, just a vast stretch of lumpy asphalt crowded with cars. Still, the place gave me the willies, and I departed as quickly as the speed bumps allowed. By the time I arrived at the restaurant, my leg was hurting, although some of this may have been psychological, because the limp was almost gone and the shin not quite so tender.

I had a small salad and a French dip sandwich—oh, okay, french fries, too. While I ate, my thoughts bopped around from the fragility of life, to the memory of Erik's fingers hard around my wrist, to the fact that I still hadn't called the insurance company about the van.

Well, skip the first two items. I had no time for either existential or romantic reverie.

On a practical level, I decided that unless I heard from Jerry Reeser or Marilyn Wylie pretty soon Robb's house would be my next stop and that I'd make my report to the insurance company from there, saving at least one car phone charge.

After my early lunch there was nothing for it but to check in with Danny and field his anxious questions about my "accident" the night before as duly reported by Harry. Only Danny had noticed my limp, so actually he got the version I'd told Erik—I think.

In the midst of all this creative deception, I did accomplish my original purpose, which was to ask for my messages. There were a few, nothing urgent and nothing from Reeser or Marilyn Wylie.

Of the people Danny reached and talked to about Kate, none had seen much of her recently, except for one woman who said she'd loaned Kate a hundred dollars and wanted to know if there was any chance of getting the money back.

"I'll keep trying," Danny said, "but after that I'm running out of things to do. If I had Mr. Sannerman's financial records I could start on those. Would you like me to hop on my bike and meet you somewhere?"

Understand that only a demon bike rider like Danny would make such an offer. I was a long way from Santa Ana.

"It's not a bad idea," I said. "The problem is I don't know for sure where I'll be. I'll have to call you."

"Well, do you want me to call the insurance company? Get the paperwork started?"

"Oh gee, thanks, no. I'd better do that myself."

I'm usually pretty up front with Danny, so why was I keeping things from him now? Somehow I'd slipped into this pattern of evasion. Mostly small, white fibs. Some selective editing here and there.

Lying's an occupational hazard for me. I can barely do my job without an occasional whopper. Still, I sensed there was more going on here, and I thought about it while I drove over to Nellie Gail.

Usually I excused my little fabrications by telling myself that I didn't want my friends to worry. But were my actions altogether altruistic? Or was it mainly that I didn't want to answer to anybody else because their concerns might slow me down?

At Robb's house I left the van on the driveway and went inside, reminded immediately of the other day when I snooped around while Robb slept, unsuspecting, on the sofa. Which made me think about the possibility that I was basically a deceitful human being with no redeemable qualities.

Gary might have a few thoughts on that one.

TWENTY

EXCEPT FOR THAT FIRST DAY when I discovered Kate's body, I had never been alone in the Sannerman house. A kind of supernatural stillness filled the rooms, a silence that makes you expect to hear the electric clock in the kitchen tick. The refrigerator motor came on, and the whir made me jump. If driving through the parking lot at the mall had given me the willies, walking into Robb's place made the hair stand up on the backs of my arms.

Everything looked the same as it had the other night when Robb had been arrested, as though that moment had been frozen in time. Our mugs were on the coffee table, mine almost full and Robb's with about two inches of ringed liquid. The tray was there with the untouched cookies. In the kitchen the cold leftover coffee in the glass carafe of the drip machine was scummed over and gave off a faint moldy, oily smell. The dishes were still in the sink, the mail piled on the counter.

Outside, leaves choked the pool, and the water was a poisonous green. The leaves and blossoms of the gazanias looked curled and shrunken, stressed by the heat of the Santa Ana winds and needing a good watering. Beyond the chain link fence, the grass in the pasture was crisp and dry, although the line of oleanders that marked the boundary with the Wylies' property looked healthy enough. Oleanders thrive on hot weather.

Kate had been sitting out there on the patio the day she died—wired on cocaine or going into withdrawal, desperate for a hit? I hadn't seen the autopsy report. Since the cause of death was obvious, I wasn't sure they would have run a tox screen. My money was on the fact that Kate was on the edge that day, trying to distract herself with gin and tonic, a swim, some sun.

I pictured her here in the kitchen, slicing limes, taking the blue ice trays from the refrigerator.

Kate always liked crushed ice, Robb had said.

I'd wondered where the killer got the hammer. Now I knew. I could see it.

Kate brings the hammer in from the garage or maybe she keeps it here. She wraps the cubes in a dish towel and smashes them into slivers. Maybe she enjoyed doing it, a small act of savagery that releases some tension. She takes her glass outside and downs the cold, bitter drink. She feels the sun burning her skin, listens to the radio. She thinks desperate thoughts. Then somebody comes. Maybe Lee Gersky—through the gate, or he rings the bell and she comes inside to answer it.

They argue, something to do with the drugs, but most likely the quarrel is also about money. The hammer lies there on the counter. He picks it up. She thinks he's fooling around, but it scares her, he scares her. She retreats to the patio, trying to escape . . .

No, she was not struck in the back of the head, running away. Why had she faced him? Maybe she thought she could calm him down, that he wasn't really capable of hitting her. This became even more

probable if it wasn't a man who held the hammer but
Tamra.

Shivering, I tried to run off the gruesome visions by
thinking about practical things. The mailbox outside
was probably full. I took a quick trip to empty it. Then
I went to make sure the pool equipment was switched
off, turned on the sprinklers, came back to clean up
the cups and dump out the coffee and stale cookies.

I knew this was busywork and in the long run probably wouldn't matter. Houses and yards—*lives*—need
constant care. This place wouldn't get it, not if Robb
stayed in jail. Which reminded me to get on with what
I'd come to do.

This time, with Robb's permission, I collected check
stubs, bank statements, credit card receipts, and
itemized telephone bills. That done I went into the
kitchen and sat on one of the bar stools to call my insurance company. I told them somebody had sideswiped me. Not exactly a lie—I just left out my
conviction that it was deliberate and not the random
action of some nutcase.

What can I say?

I'm incorrigible.

I've had big claims in the recent past for medical
and the property damage at my office. However, my
vehicles had gone unscathed. Although the damage
was not my fault, the agent told me I'd still have to
fork over the five hundred deductible if I wanted the
van fixed.

On that cheery note I called Marilyn Wylie at her
office. She was still not back from lunch. I might as
well save Danny a long bike ride. I turned off the

sprinklers, locked up, and was more than happy to take Robb's financial records back to the office.

I MANAGED TO SNEAK in undetected past Harry. Danny had left a note saying he had gone to lunch. I worked my way through a small stack of phone messages, batting my usual .500. I did pick up a missing heir assignment that Danny could work on. He'd acquired a database that contained every telephone directory in the United States, which was a great place to start.

Nothing from either Reeser or Marilyn Wylie. I tried Reeser again. Either he wasn't home or he wasn't answering. At Marilyn's office, the receptionist said Mrs. Wylie still wasn't back. Did I want to leave a message? I did.

The door in the outer office opened and Danny sang out, "It's just me." He came in, unfastening his bicycle helmet. "You didn't do the interviews?"

"Nope, no luck."

I gave him the details on the missing heir, and he promised to get on it right away. He gestured to Robb's financial records, which were spread out on my desk. "Anything interesting?"

"I just started."

"How's the ankle?"

"Fine."

I flipped pages and tried to look distracted.

"When you have a minute, there's something—" He hesitated. "Never mind. I'll tell you later."

He went off to his computer. I lectured myself sternly on the virtues of honesty and setting a good example.

AN HOUR LATER I'd gone through Robb's stuff, flagging a few things with Post-its for follow-up. However, for the most part, the records yielded patterns but little else. For example: lots of frequent checks written at the supermarket at one or two hundred dollars a pop; lots of advances on the credit cards. Kate's habit had been cash and carry, as far as I could tell. She hadn't been paying by check.

I put everything into an expandable folder and reached for the phone. Still no answer at Reeser's. Marilyn's office now reported she might not be coming back today, sounding vague on why this was. She might or might not be at the design center. I took a chance and called her home number.

Wonder of wonders—she answered the phone.

"Mrs. Wylie? It's Delilah West. We spoke last week about Tamra."

"Oh, yes. The private eye Ben hired. I hear you didn't find my daughter."

This didn't seem to upset her. As a matter of fact, she sounded happy about it in a malicious sort of way. *Ha, ha, Ben Wylie,* I could almost hear her saying, *not so smart after all, you and your dumb detective.*

"You don't sound worried," I said. "Has Tamra been in touch with you?"

"No—not that it's any of your business. I'm very busy, Ms. West, so tell me what you want."

"I need to talk to you, Mrs. Wylie," I said. "It's important. I'd like to come by your house."

"Certainly not. I came home to do some paperwork," she said irritably. "I don't have time to waste on you. Anyway, we have nothing to discuss."

Click.

I sat with the receiver in my hand for a second, considering, hung up, and grabbed my purse. In the outer office, Danny, glued to his computer, gave a start when I walked in. He reminded me of a kid caught with his hand in the cookie jar. I didn't look too closely, but the stuff on the computer screen did not appear to be telephone listings.

Never mind.

I didn't want to know.

"I'm going to talk to Marilyn Wylie," I said. "I'll check in later."

"Bye, boss. Good luck." He gave me a smile that was just a little phony around the edges.

Great.

I've corrupted Danny, too.

MARILYN'S ADDRESS was in Corona del Mar three blocks off the ocean, a small house, old but beautifully kept, freshly painted in white and a soft gray-blue. The yard was dominated by an enormous coral tree. Hot pink and scarlet impatiens bordered the walk that led to the door.

I'd broken all the speed limits—that is to say, I'd kept up with the rest of the traffic—getting down here. Marilyn had said she was doing paperwork. I hoped it was enough to keep her occupied and at home. There was a white Lexus on the driveway, a good sign.

I rang the bell and waited, rang again. Finally, I heard footsteps, and a woman called through the door, "Yes? Who is it?"

"Mrs. Wylie? I'm from the design center? About those samples?"

"What?"

I deliberately pitched my voice too low to be heard clearly. "About the paint samples? Somebody spilled coffee and the order got messed up and—"

The door opened.

"What is this? Something about paint? I didn't talk to anybody about paint."

Marilyn Wylie looked like a woman who had been plagued by interruptions and confrontations since she got out of bed this morning. Our phone conversation hadn't helped and now I was going to make her bad day a whole lot worse.

Her slim body was taut, her sharp features set in lines of aggravation. I suspected even her hair was giving her fits. Short and ash blond, the asymmetrical cut hung limply, a strand dangling near her eyes. She wore a short black skirt, a silk blouse in a black and brown tribal print, and high-heeled shoes.

Not my idea of a comfortable work-at-home outfit, but maybe she was going out again.

I judged her to be about forty, which meant Benjamin Wylie was a good fifteen years older, and that she had been fairly young when Tamra was born.

"Mrs. Wylie, I'm Delilah West," I said. "Can I come in for a minute?"

I stepped up as though I expected to be invited in. She retreated slightly, but blocked the doorway.

"You said you were from the design center."

"Yes, sorry. I didn't think you'd let me in if I told you who I really was."

"Well, you're right about that."

She tried to close the door, but I had my foot inside and my body against the wooden panel. She pushed and I resisted. A touch of fear mixed with her annoyance.

"Here, you, what are you doing?"

"Are you too busy feuding with your ex-husband to worry about your daughter, Mrs. Wylie? For God's sake, she's with a man who's probably a murderer."

"Lee?" She looked at me like I was stark raving mad, but her pressure on the door eased off.

"So Tamra *is* with him, and she's been in touch with you, hasn't she?" I asked. "Come on, Mrs. Wylie. Talk to me."

Somewhere in the house the phone began to ring. I took advantage of her momentary distraction to shove against the door and step inside.

She moved away with ill grace, brushing back her hair and saying, "Oh, all right. I have to get the phone. Just wait in there."

She indicated a living area off the entry hall and hurried off, her heels clicking on the ceramic tile. The room had bone-white walls—even the brick fireplace was painted the same color—a pale cognac carpet, and two white love seats with some throw pillows in a jade green and bright blue print, the furniture scaled for the small area.

Before I could sit down, Marilyn was back to say the phone call was for me. Danny was the only person who knew where I was.

"We haven't been coming up with anything on Tamra Wylie," he said. "So I started thinking. You know Mr. Wylie withdrew the authorization before we found out about any ATM transactions, but—"

"But you've taken a peek anyway," I finished, remembering what I'd seen on his computer screen.

"Yes, and she did use her card. She used it twice right after she left, that same day and the next. I checked the locations and guess what?"

The two machines where the card had been used to obtain the maximum two hundred dollars in cash per day were both on Pacific Coast Highway, very near to Marilyn Wylie's address.

TWENTY-ONE

I HAD TAKEN DANNY'S CALL in the kitchen. Marilyn hovered nearby. On a table in an adjoining eating area, I could see a laptop computer and a tidy stack of papers. The kitchen itself had been modernized, the cabinets painted white with glass inserts. It took a brave woman to let you look into the insides of her kitchen cabinets, or maybe just one who was compulsively neat.

As soon as I hung up, Marilyn led the way back into the living room and perched on the edge of one of the love seats, giving her hair an angry swipe and saying, "This is all such nonsense. You've got that boy blown up into some kind of bogeyman, perfectly ridiculous, as if he'd kidnapped Tamra and dragged her off someplace."

"And you know he didn't."

"*Yes*, because they—" She broke off and glared at me.

"Because they came here," I finished for her. "Look, I know Tamra used two different ATM machines in this area. I can talk to your neighbors if I have to—"

"All *right*," she snapped. "Of course she came here. After that awful scene with Ben, where else would she go?"

"You told her father you hadn't seen or heard from her."

"Well, Tamra didn't want him to know where she was. He treats her like she's about ten years old. The man does nothing but hassle her. You've no idea."

"Oh, I think I do," I said. "Mr. Wylie found her in bed with Lee and blew his top. I'm not a fan of your husband's, but this time he had a point."

"Ex-husband." Her look lumped me in with the rest of the misguided old fogeys. "So she's having sex— well, my, my, how shocking. It's the nineties, for goodness' sake. And of *course* Ben doesn't think Lee's good enough. So the boy's a little rough around the edges, so what? Ben just can't accept the fact that Tamra's not daddy's little girl anymore. She's old enough to make her own decisions."

"Judging by the company she keeps, she's not doing such a hot job. Where did they go when they left here, Mrs. Wylie? I'm assuming they did leave?"

"If you must know," she said stiffly, "they left the next morning. Tamra made me promise not to tell her father where they were going, so I'm certainly not going to tell you."

"I guess you don't know," I said. "I don't work for Mr. Wylie anymore. So he won't hear it from me."

She looked bewildered. "Then who are you working for?"

"Robb Sannerman."

"Oh, great. You're working for a murderer, and you come in here calling poor Lee names?"

"The last I heard," I said, "our system considers a man innocent until proven guilty. As for poor Lee—let me tell you a little bit about him."

I didn't pull any punches. I told her about Lee's good buddies down at the Hilltop Apartments, about his DUI and his assault arrest, about the drugs and Kate's addiction and how I thought it was all connected.

She sat and stared at me, her skin going pale, about the same ashy color as her hair.

"Here's what I think happened the day Kate died," I went on. "After Ben found Lee and Tamra and the argument started, Lee ducked out. I think he went next door, and Kate started in on him. They argued and he killed her. Then he went off and met Tamra someplace and they came here."

I didn't tell her this was only one of the scenarios I'd thought of.

"No." She shook her head. "No, that's impossible. I would have noticed something—I mean, Tamra was upset because of the fight with Ben, but Lee—no, I don't believe it."

"Maybe you don't, but the police haven't discounted Lee entirely. They put out an APB on him and your daughter."

Yeah, I know, my usual distortion of the facts. Like I said, part of the job.

"I don't understand," Marilyn said. "If they already made an arrest—"

"Maybe they have new information. I have to tell you, Mrs. Wylie, if you and Tamra have been helping this guy and he does get arrested, well, aiding and abetting is a pretty serious charge."

"But we *didn't*—I mean, how would we know? *You* don't even know for sure what happened to Kate. You're just trying to scare me."

But not succeeding, not yet.

I said, "So after everything I've told you, you still think Tamra's off having wonderful sex with her boyfriend with the added bonus of driving her father crazy—"

"Yes," she said defiantly.

"Then you've talked to her since she left?"

Suddenly she wasn't so certain anymore. "They don't have a phone up there, but she—she's okay."

"You know that for a fact?"

"All *right,*" she said. "A friend of mine has a house at Arrowhead. That's where they went. Go talk to Tamra. Talk to Lee. Then you'll see how wrong you are about all of this."

As BAD AS THE traffic is in Orange County, it's nothing compared to the Riverside freeway leaving the basin at 4:30 P.M. Because land is cheaper, lower-priced developments in places like Corona and Moreno Valley have lured young families, creating new bedroom communities a mere two-hour commute from L.A. The problem is there are only a few main arteries to handle the commuters, each one badly in need of a quadruple bypass.

Inching along in the homeward-bound rush I thought about that two-hour drive-time figure and decided it must be a conservative estimate. I had plenty of time to call Danny and tell him that I had found out where Tamra and Lee had gone.

"Great," he said. "So now the police can pick them up."

"Well . . ."

I was tempted to lie, I'll admit it. While I was deciding, Danny, alarmed, said, "You're going up there?"

"Yes, I am. I owe it to my client to talk to them first. I know guys like Lee. If they see any kind of criminal charge coming, they scream for a public defender and then clam up."

"You'll be careful."

"You bet." Anticipating the long drive, I'd taken off the Beretta and put it and its holster in the glove box, but I wasn't going to leave the van without the weapon. "Tell you what. Where will you be at ten o'clock? I'll check in."

"I'll be at home."

"Okay. You'll hear from me. If you don't, then you can sound the alarm."

"All right, I will."

From the tone of Danny's voice, I thought I'd damn well better remember to call him.

AFTER THAT I HAD more time to kill, except there was nobody else I needed or wanted to talk to. No point in calling Jerry Reeser back now that I knew where Lee and Tamra were—depending, of course, on what I found in Lake Arrowhead. Too difficult to get hold of Robb; anyway, I wanted to wait until I had something concrete to report.

So there I was, my mind in free fall. I thought about Erik; well, I do. It's a hormonal thing, like the way men are supposed to think about sex every few minutes. Mostly I just worried over the case, turning things this way and that, trying to see every angle, wondering what I was missing.

I'd convinced myself that Lee and Tamra were linked to Kate's death, but there was always the possibility that I was wrong. The whole thing might just be coincidence, nothing more, one big tangent leading away from what had really happened that day. After I talked to the two of them, I might be right back where I'd started, both Robb and I running out of time.

BY 6:45 I WAS FINALLY on State Route 18, snaking my way up the side of the San Bernardino range on a ten-mile run of four-lane road that was fast in spite of the curves. Or, all things being relative, maybe it just seemed fast after rush hour on the freeway. The mountainsides were covered with low-growing scrub, yucca, and Spanish broom, looking burned and brown after the summer heat.

I'd made one stop to fill the gas tank. Dinner was, once again, minimart cuisine for sustenance only: a hot dog, coffee, and some soft ice cream. I'd worry about my vitamins tomorrow. Since the drive was bothering my sore muscles, I had used the last of the coffee to wash down some Motrin.

Where the road narrows to two lanes, a sign reminded me it was called Rim of the World Highway. This section had sheer drop-offs and the sunset view toward L.A. would have been spectacular if it hadn't been for the layer of smog covering the basin.

Some scrubby trees appeared, then quickly the growth turned into a forest. At an altitude of about five thousand feet, huge ponderosa and sugar pine grew in thick stands mixed with cedar, spruce, and live oak. Twilight was rapidly fading into darkness as I made the turnoff toward Lake Arrowhead.

After ski season ends, the two resort areas in the San Bernardino Mountains are distinctly different. Big Bear is T-shirts and postcards, RV gridlock in the summer, beer bellies and kids with sticky fingers. Arrowhead is antiques, arts and crafts, and old Hollywood money. The lake is privately owned, the shoreline almost completely developed. The oldest, smallest house on the water could set you back three hundred big ones.

Just at the entrance to Arrowhead Village I turned right to follow the lake. However, I'd been up here before and remembered the small business area. No hodge-podge free enterprise was allowed in there. Everything had been built to spec: red-roofed buildings, clean and orderly, that looked as though they were intended for some English town.

Away from the lake things were a lot looser. Rustic cabins were tucked away in the woods up skinny, winding roads. Tamra was staying in one of these cabins instead of a mansion with its own boat dock.

Marilyn Wylie had given me directions, but I missed the turn and had to double back, straining to read the street signs in the rapidly failing light. Once I found the street, I crawled along looking for the house. Some places had numbers, most didn't. The cabin belonging to Marilyn's friend was, obviously, among the unmarked.

I finally found one that seemed approximately in the right spot and more or less matched Marilyn's description and thought I was damn lucky to do so.

The dark wood siding and the shake roof seemed to vanish into the dense trees, and there was no outside lighting at all, just the glow of the windows to illuminate the small building. I swung the van into a narrow driveway. I couldn't see Tamra's Integra, but then a whole convoy of tanks could have been out there, unseen, in the blackness of the woods.

With the lights off, it was very dark in the van too. I'd turned the heat on a few miles back, so I knew it would be cold outside. Fortunately, my zippered sweatshirt was handy. I put it on, changed my sandals for sneakers, then unlocked the glove box and took out the Beretta, aware that my heart rate had accelerated just a tick.

In the middle of clipping the holster to my waistband in back, I stopped, took the mini-automatic from the holster and slipped it into the sweatshirt pocket instead. Then I took out the .38 and stuck *that* in my waistband.

Jesus, talk about paranoid. But with all the men in my life urging me to be careful, somehow two guns didn't seem too many.

Armed to the teeth, I got out of the van and headed for the cabin.

TWENTY-TWO

A SHORT FLIGHT of stone steps led to a cement stoop at the door of the cabin. I climbed up, wondering how I was going to talk my way inside. Just then a dim amber light came on above the door, an unshaded bulb, the kind that's not supposed to attract bugs, and the door opened, spilling more light and the sound of a television program laugh track.

At least I could stop worrying about Tamra Wylie's safety. She stood looking out at me, frowning, her mother's daughter, in looks anyway, except for the mass of dark hair, like her father's must have been before it went gray. She'd been expecting somebody, but I wasn't that person.

"Tamra? Hi," I said quickly before she could back away from a stranger and shut the door in my face.

"Hello." The wariness remained. "Sorry—do I know you from somewhere?"

"No. I'm Delilah West. Your mother told me you were here. Brrr, it's getting cold. Could I come in?"

She hesitated, then stepped back and held the door open.

Another burst of canned laughter erupted from the television set. A sitcom—I had no idea which one. They all seem to be made from the same script with interchangeable characters.

After seeing the house in Corona del Mar, I was sure Marilyn had not helped her friend decorate the cabin.

Some kind of rough wood paneled the walls. The furniture was Early American, sturdy maple with cushions that featured ducks in the dark blue and burgundy print and bore signs of long, hard use: water rings and cigarette burns on the wood, oily stains on the upholstery at head level.

An open can of Pepsi added another ring to the coffee table. A bag of Doritos sat next to the can, ripped open along the entire length of the package, exuding the smell of corn and cheese.

Tamra's body, clad in jeans and a plaid shirt, had the skeletal thinness that seems to be every young woman's goal these days, although I did see a slight curve at the hip and bosom. Holed up here, maybe she'd gained a couple of pounds, not surprising if her current choice of snacks was any example of her diet this week. It also looked as though she was eating alone.

Checking, I said, "Is Lee here?" I had to raise my voice a little over the noise of the TV.

"No," she said shortly and slouched down on the couch with that combination of indolence and elegance that only young people her age can manage.

I sat, uninvited, in a platform rocker across from her. One thing about Early American, it's longer on comfort than it is on looks. Or rather it would have been comfortable if it hadn't been for the .38 making a great big lump in my back.

"Miss—West?" Tamra asked.

"Delilah."

"Delilah," she repeated, but she said it as though she was humoring me, a generation gap yawning between us. "Are you a friend of Dorothy Weinstaub?"

Marilyn hadn't mentioned the owner's name, but Weinstaub seemed like a good guess. Well, I was down to it. What version of the truth did I use this time? I'd thought about it on the way up, deciding, as usual to wing it.

While I hesitated, the TV blared another round of hilarity. I gestured to it and said, "Could we have that off?"

It took a second for her to realize that I was suggesting we didn't need the background noise. Her look consigned me to the doddering old folks who couldn't, as Danny describes it, multiplex, but she shrugged and got up to switch off the set.

While she was doing this, I was busy weighing Marilyn's opinion that Tamra was going to be hopping mad when she found out her father had hired me against something Elena had said about Tamra and Benjamin Wylie: *I think if she cannot get him to notice the good thing then she always does the bad.*

When Tamra sat back down on the sofa, I said, "I'm not a friend of Mrs. Weinstaub. I'm a private detective. Your father hired me to find you."

Well, it wasn't the whole truth.

Big surprise.

"You're kidding," Tamra said, astonished and not at all displeased at that much attention from her father.

"No, I'm not kidding. He was very worried, especially after what happened next door. You heard about Mrs. Sannerman?"

"It was on the news," she said. "I mean, I couldn't believe it. Kate might have been, like, *dead* while I was still there. And then Robb got arrested. That was so totally mind-blowing. I knew they didn't get along, but I mean—God!"

Okay, check off one of my scenarios. If Tamra had wielded that hammer, she was one honey of a little actress.

"Actually," I said, "the police think it happened about the time you left. They've been looking for you and Lee, too."

"They have? Why?"

"They want to talk to anybody who was around that day. When do you expect Lee back, by the way?"

"Soon, I guess. I still don't get why the police would want to talk to us."

"I imagine they would like to ask a few questions about what the two of you saw."

"Like what? God, I sure didn't see anything. Daddy and I—I don't know how much he told you—"

"I know he found you and Lee together, and there was a big fight."

"Yeah, well, you can imagine. It was pretty intense. I just, like, slammed out of there and took off."

"What about Lee? He left before you did."

"I don't blame him. I mean my dad just totally freaked."

There was a little gleam of satisfaction in her eyes at the memory. I doubted she would ever admit she planned the incident, but at some level she had wanted it to happen.

"What did Lee do after he left your house?"

"What do you mean, what did he do?" she asked, instantly suspicious, Benjamin Wylie to a tee.

"Well, he didn't have a car," I said. "And how was he to know how long you and your dad would be arguing? He knew Kate. Maybe he decided to wait over there."

"No! No way. You mean like he might have seen her body? God!"

"She might have still been alive," I pointed out, at least when he arrived.

"Well, he didn't go over there. He wouldn't have anyway. He hung out around the corner and waited." Another suspicious look. "You ask an awful lot of questions. What do you want to know about all that stuff for?"

I shrugged. "Just curious. It's an intriguing case, don't you think so? I mean, she lived right next door to you." I helped myself to a couple of Doritos, gestured to her pop can, and said, "Could I have one of those? I didn't eat much for dinner."

She went out to the kitchen and brought back two cans. She didn't do this cheerfully, but then Tamra did not strike me as a cheerful person.

I thanked her and took a swallow. Breaking bread together, or in this case sipping Pepsi, usually puts things on a more congenial basis. I listened for the sound of a car, Lee returning, while I was being sociable.

"I understand you and Kate were friends," I said. "That you used to help her with Goldy. Beautiful horse. Your dad showed me a picture."

"She knew me," she said. "All I had to do was go to the fence and call." There was sadness in the dark eyes, quickly shuttered. "Kate sold her."

"That must have been very hard for her to do."

"I don't know. Who could tell? Kate got to be such a coke head." She took a chip and stared at it. Put it back and drank some Pepsi.

"That's what I heard," I said. "Such a shame. I understand she went through all their money."

"She sold her jewelry—this totally beautiful sapphire ring that belonged to her mom. She even took all her kitchen stuff and some furniture and had a friend sell it at her garage sale." Tamra jumped up and went over to the window, pulling aside a ruffled curtain to peer into the darkness. "You said my mom told you I was here."

"That's right. She did."

"Figures. I never can count on her. She promised my dad wouldn't find me."

"She hadn't heard from you, Tamra. She was getting worried, too."

Tamra came back to plop down on the sofa. "Well, she knows there's no phone—isn't that the stupidest thing? Mrs. Weinstaub says she just uses her cellular—like nobody else might want to make a call. Lee wants me to take off with him. My folks'll be lucky if I don't do it. Don't think you're going to make me go back with you. I don't care what my dad paid you."

"Hey, I can't force you. Your parents wanted to know you're okay. And you are—so far."

"What's that supposed to mean?"

"This past week while I was looking for you, I found out a lot about your boyfriend, not very nice things."

"Oh, great. Like I really care what *you* think about him."

"He has some wonderful friends," I persisted. "Ever meet them? Randy Beaumont?" I named the other two. "They deal dope, Tamra. Lee probably does too."

"He does not!"

"No? I can tell you he sold to Kate."

"Oh, yeah, well, *Kate*. He was doing her a favor. I mean, come on. It's not like Lee is some scumbag selling dope to little kids. He didn't even charge her any extra—well, not much anyway." She broke off to give me an accusing stare. "Oh, I see what you're doing. You're trying to make it seem like Lee had something to do with Kate's murder just because he felt sorry for her. Well, she had lots of other people selling the stuff to her. And another thing, Lee heard some guy was supplying her for, you know, *sex*."

"Who was it?"

"He didn't tell me. Ask Lee if you want all the disgusting details."

"I'd like to. Where is he, Tamra?"

"Out. I don't know. He went to meet somebody."

That cold chill of premonition was back, only this time I wasn't going to ignore it.

"I don't suppose he told you who this person was?"

She shook her head, jumped up, and paced around some more. "Some guy who owes Lee money. Lee's been bugging him all week. We could've had a thousand dollars from my ATM card by now, but Lee said

Daddy might find us if we used it up here. Like I really cared. But Lee said we should lay low and stay out of Daddy's face for a while. He said as soon as he gets the money we'll go to Vegas.''

She shoved her hands in her pockets and treated the room to a resentful stare as though she'd been forced to come here. ''God, he knows how I hate this boring place, but he got all macho on me and wouldn't let me go with him. Probably the guy never showed up, and Lee's getting totally drunk. I swear if he smashes up my car, I'll just kill him.''

Talk about your cold shivers.

''Tell you what,'' I said. ''Why don't I go look for him? There must be someplace you guys hang out. If he's drunk, I won't let him drive. I'll bring him home.''

''Yeah? Good luck.''

Jackets hung on a peg by the door. She grabbed a blue windbreaker and said, ''I'd better go with you.''

''No, not a good idea. What if we miss him and he comes back here to find you gone?''

''So what if he does?'' She gave me one of her sideways looks, condemning me for feminist heresy. ''Are we going or not?''

I didn't see any way of making her stay behind, short of hog-tieing her, and, on second thought, what if the guy came back to the cabin with Lee? That possibility certainly generated a few unsettling scenarios.

We left the house and set off into one of the blackest nights I've ever seen. The moon was up. Some high cirrus and the tall trees did a damn good job blocking out the starlight. There was a solidity to the darkness.

My headlights cut through like laser beams with no spillover to illuminate the roadside.

We went to several places—Lee's tastes, I'd bet. None of them were in the village. Mostly they ran to smoky little taverns with lots of rough-sawn wood, wavy mirrors, dim lighting, and country rock on the music system. Once in a while I could see the lake, so I could fix it as a reference point.

Finally, somewhere near the dam, we left the main road and drove off down a narrow lane with the trees practically meeting overhead. The lane came to a dead end in a parking lot in front of yet another rustic saloon.

There was one lone light pole in the lot, casting a pale white glow. Plenty enough to see Tamra's Integra and right next to it a big old Ford 350, dark gray with a cargo net instead of a tailgate and a nice unchipped windshield that I'd lay money was newly installed.

TWENTY-THREE

I PARKED NEXT TO the Ford truck. As soon as we stopped rolling, Tamra reached for the door handle.

I grabbed her arm and said, "Wait. We have to talk."

"What? That's my car. I thought you were so hot to see Lee."

"Listen, I've been straight with you as far as it goes, but there's a lot of things I haven't told you, and I don't have time to explain it all now. Just trust me when I tell you that the guy Lee's meeting is very likely the man who killed Kate Sannerman."

"God," she whispered, gawking at me, her mouth and eyes rounding even more as I took the .38 from my waistband and checked to see that it was fully loaded.

"Stay here," I said. "Lock the door."

"You're scaring me," she said.

"I intend to. I'll leave the keys in the ignition, and there's the car phone. Anything happens, call the police and get the hell out of here."

She nodded. Her face looked pale in the van's interior light as I got out. I stuck the gun back in my waistband under the zippered sweatshirt, leaving the sweatshirt open. Then I went around the front of the truck. I knew I wasn't wrong, but I checked the bumper and found a streak of blue paint that had to be from the side of my van.

"Gotcha," I whispered.

I ordered myself to stay loose as I walked over to the tavern, but I could feel the tension building in my body and the adrenaline kicking in. One good thing. The aches and pains had vanished. Nothing like nature's good old fight-or-flight drug, better than Motrin any day.

The saloon looked as though it might have once been a private home. A veranda ran all the way around, and this entry level was well above the ground, the way houses were built when there was less paving and a lot more mud. Steps went up at the side, themselves attached to a board sidewalk that edged the back of the parking lot.

Where the sidewalk made a right angle off into the woods, a small wooden sign was affixed to a low post. The sign read BOAT DOCK, and an arrow pointed the way. We must be closer to the water than I had thought. Or maybe the dock was on one of the many inlets that services the lake, allowing customers to come over in a boat for their Miller on draft. Voices drifted up from that direction, too far away to distinguish any words. A breeze rustled the pine needles, bringing an over-powering smell of pitch mixed with a hint of vanilla.

Under my feet the stairs were slightly concave from wear and creaked with each step. I could hear music from the tavern, muffled to its basic elements of drumbeats with a counterpoint of laughter. A big picture window was decorated with beer signs. SCREAMIN' EDDIE'S was painted on the glass.

Just as I got to the door it opened, and two men came out. Neither of them was Lee. The odor of booze and cigarette smoke wafted out to mix with the piney scent of the woods. I went inside, my senses on full alert, doing a quick scan in light levels barely brighter than the parking lot.

One glance confirmed that the place had once been a house. It had a feel of something built in the twenties with high ceilings and small, functional rooms. The interior walls had not been removed entirely, just cut down to half the original height, giving the feel of lots of alcoves and corners. Immediately to the right a bar was lined with some heavy wooden stools. Small tables and ladder-back chairs were scattered throughout the rest of the place. The floors were bare and splintery, the walls covered in antique signs and old license plates.

I estimated the crowd at twenty-five people, not bad for a weekday this time of year. There was a poker game going over in one corner. Off to the left in one of the alcoves, tables had been pushed back to form a dance floor where several couples were making a sloppy, drunken, happy attempt at line dancing. Three men sat at the bar watching, the heels of their cowboy boots hooked on the stool rungs.

Lee wasn't there.

I let out a pent-up breath I hadn't even realized I was holding. One of the dancers stumbled, and they all whooped with laughter. I eased over to the bar. The nearest man of the trio sitting there did a quick assessment, looked like he might say something, changed his mind, and went back to watching the frivolity in the alcove. I don't know what he saw on my face, but the bartender noticed it, too.

He said, "What can I get you?" his voice neutral and his eyes alert and watchful.

"I'm looking for somebody." I described Lee for him. "He was meeting another fellow."

"Yeah, I saw him. Hung around by himself for a while, then his friend showed up and they left."

"When was that?"

"Maybe half-hour ago."

"This other guy—what did he look like?"

"I don't know, ma'am. I didn't pay much attention. It was kinda busy. You havin' a drink?"

"No, thanks."

I went outside, hugging the building and staying in the shadows on the way back to the stairs. Tamra's car and the truck were still in the lot with my van parked alongside. I couldn't see Tamra inside the van at first until she sat up straight.

Coming off the stairs and down the wooden sidewalk, I could hear voices again from the direction of the boat dock. Men's voices, stridently angry, although I still couldn't make out what was being said.

"Delilah?"

Tamra had the door open and was calling across the parking lot. Probably could hear her all the way to the village. I signaled *no, stop, go back,* but instead she got out and slammed the door.

Muttering curses, I hurried to intercept her. Maybe my earlier warning hadn't been graphic enough because she had shaken off her fear. She looked belligerent and stubborn, which shouldn't have surprised me knowing her mom and dad.

"What's going on?" she demanded. "Did you find him?"

"No. Get back in the van."

"I want to talk to Lee. I know what you're doing. You're trying to make a big deal out of this to scare me into going home. Lee's just meeting this guy who owes him money, that's all—" She broke off, turning to listen. The voices from the dock were very loud now, raised in a violent argument.

"Oh, God," Tamra said, starting off toward the board sidewalk. "That's Lee. He *has* been drinking."

"Tamra, wait." I hurried to catch up with her and grabbed her arm. "For God's sake—"

Gunshots roared off in the woods and a man screamed. Tamra cried, "Lee! That was Lee!" and struck out wildly at me. She connected with my sore arm. The blow produced enough pain so my grip slackened. She eeled away and took off.

She'd only gone a step or two before I was running after her, fumbling with the .38 and pulling it free of the elastic waistband as I ran. Just as she reached the sidewalk, a man bolted from the trees, coming at us down the walk, his footsteps pounding the wood.

Tamra, light on her feet, ignored my frantic shout and widened the gap between us. She went two more running strides before she realized the man was not Lee, a split second before I recognized him. She made a panicked skid, trying to stop and turn back.

I crouched and leveled my gun, shouted, "Tamra, get down!"

But it was too late.

Jerry Reeser grabbed her, his arm snaking around her waist, lifting her off her feet and pulling her back against him. She yelped in pain and surprise.

"Shut up, shut the fuck *up*," he said. "I'll kill you just like your boyfriend."

He came a step closer, holding her with his left arm. I could see the gun in his right hand pressed into her ribs, some kind of 9 mm automatic. My hands were shaking so badly I could barely keep from dropping my own weapon.

"D-D-Delilah—" There was stark terror in Tamra's wail.

"Put it down." Reeser's voice was hoarse, charged with a crazy urgency. "I'll shoot her, I'll fucking shoot her—"

"All right," I said.

"Now! *Do* it!"

"Okay, Jerry. Stay calm." I went down on my heels and laid the .38 on the sidewalk, then slowly got up.

The weird lighting cast his face in shadows that deepened the lines carved in his cheeks and gave a gleam of madness to his eyes.

"Hands—I wanta see your hands. The gun—kick it away."

I did what he said, sending my weapon skidding off the sidewalk into the weedy darkness.

A man had come out on the veranda at Screamin' Eddie's. He yelled down, "Hey, what's goin' on? Somebody shootin' out there?"

"One word," Reeser hissed. "I'll kill her. Think it was firecrackers," he called up to the guy on the veranda.

"Sounded like a gun to me. Everything all right, ma'am?"

The bartender.

"Fine," I said, hoping he could read the falseness and fear in my voice. "Everything's fine."

The man stood there for a second or two, then went back inside. Tamra whimpered softly like a small, terrified puppy.

"Walk," Reeser ordered. "Over to the truck."

I went ahead of him and Tamra, thinking about my .38. All the times I could never get to the damn thing when I needed it and the one time I have it in my hand, I lose it right away.

Never mind.

Because it had served a purpose, after all. Jerry thought I was unarmed. He hadn't searched me. Well, it might have been a little difficult to do that what with hanging on to Tamra, but I don't think it had even crossed his mind. Now all I could do was hope it wouldn't.

I thought back to the cops on stakeout at Hilltop Apartments, how they had listened to my description of the truck and never connected it to Reeser, how I really was going to have their asses as soon as I had the chance. A little voice whispered *If you ever have a chance,* but this was not something I could afford to consider.

Some more people came out of Eddie's. I could hear excited voices. Maybe the bartender hadn't believed us after all.

"Move," Reeser said frantically. "We're going in through the passenger side. You first, Delilah. You drive."

"Not if that thing's got a stick shift," I said. "I can't drive a stick."

The truth was, I'd learned on my dad's old Karmann Ghia with four on the floor, but I was hoping to sell him on the lie because I thought I might have an edge if we were in the van. Not much of an edge, still, I know how the van handled and there was a phone if I could figure out a way to use it. However, I guess I hadn't practiced my lying skills quite enough.

He said, "Don't fuck with me, lady. I bet you could drive an eighteen-wheeler if you wanted to."

The guys from Eddie's were now pounding down the steps and heading out toward the boat dock. Flashlight beams lanced the darkness.

"Get in," Reeser said. "Let's just fucking *do* it."

I climbed up into the truck cab and slid under the wheel. Reeser shoved Tamra in quickly, slamming the door and settling himself by the window. He passed me the keys with his left hand, then kept the arm around Tamra's shoulders, squeezing her tightly. I really, really hoped he kept that arm up there, because if he decided to hold her around the waist instead, he'd be up against that small lump in my sweatshirt pocket.

"No fucking around, you hear me?" he said. "You screw up, she's dead meat."

Tamra's body was touching mine. I could feel her trembling. My own hands were shaking, so I didn't have to pretend that I was having trouble getting the key in the ignition. And it had been a while since I'd used a manual transmission. I ground the gears; the truck lurched and died on the first attempt—only slightly faked.

"Hurry up!" Reeser cried.

I took as long as I dared getting the truck rolling. Just as we left the small lot, I saw flashing beams in the mirror—the men coming back from the dock. Reeser saw it too and shouted more threats, the words broken and almost incoherent.

The truck had stiff shocks, so it was already bouncing on the patchy pavement, but he ordered, "Faster." We rocketed through the dark woods, the trees whipping by much too close. I slowed to turn onto the main road, and once on it, I didn't accelerate back to the breakneck speed.

"What are you doing?" he said. "Move."

"You want us to get stopped?" I asked. "Or maybe you'd like me to wrap this sucker around a tree. You want out of this, you're going to have to calm down."

"Can't get out," he said. "Didn't you hear me? Lee's dead."

Tamra gave a little bleat of despair.

"I couldn't help it," Reeser said. "You think I wanted to kill him? He kept shoving me and saying he wanted the money. Five thousand dollars—I told him on the phone there was no way, but he wouldn't listen."

It was chilly in the truck, and all he had on was jeans and a T-shirt, but his face shone with sweat.

"I thought if I came up here and talked to him, but it took so long with the windshield and then the traffic and by the time I found the place, he was already so ripped, and he kept pushing me, and—and—"

"So it was really just an accident," I said. "You want to think about this carefully, Jerry. Right now, well, the bartender will back up your story that Lee was drinking. And, Jesus, the man was arrested once for assaulting a cop while he was drunk. So the two of you had an argument; he got violent. You pulled the gun to defend yourself, and he jumped you. That could work Jerry. A good attorney could make it work. But only if you let us go."

"Oh, sure. What am I—crazy?"

"No, you're smart, but you're running scared and not thinking straight. We stop right now and you give it up, you can say you lost control. You panicked. You never meant to hurt us, and you prove it by turning us loose."

I thought something changed then: a slight relaxing of his shoulders, a slowing of his breathing, like maybe he was listening to reason. Then a siren wailed in the distance. The sound was like punching a fire alarm.

"Pull over!" he screamed. "Turn. In there. In the trees."

When I didn't follow his orders quickly enough, he balled a fist and brought it down on my shoulder. Pain flashed down my arm and my hand went numb. I hung on to the wheel with the other hand, fighting the bucking truck, braking. Branches slapped the window. We scraped a tree trunk.

Tamra began crying, "Oh God Oh God Oh God," over and over.

The truck shuddered to a stop.

"Lights, the goddamned *lights*." Reeser reached over to turn them off himself, using his right hand to do it, the hand that held the gun. He leaned forward away from Tamra—moving the gun away from her to stab at the switch.

The opportunity was there. Not a perfect opportunity. Tamra was close; we were all jammed tightly in the cab. He might use the gun and bullets could ricochet. Still, I would have done it, grabbed the Beretta and shot the son of a bitch.

The problem was I couldn't.

My fingers tingled, the feeling returning but not nearly fast enough and no way in hell could I slip my hand into my pocket before he had settled back with the gun in Tamra's ribs.

We sat in the dark truck while a patrol car flashed past on the road. The siren blared, then made a Doppler shift and quickly diminished in volume until it was just an echo, and the main sounds were Tamra's mantra and Reeser's ragged breathing.

Cops can act fast, but only if they are convinced of the urgency of a threat. Would the men from Screamin' Eddie's realize that Reeser had taken us away in the truck? Would the bartender remember I had asked about Lee and the man he was meeting, that I hadn't even known what the man looked like, so why should I go off with a stranger?

Time—it would take time to sort all that out, and—what time was it anyway? If there was a clock in the cab I hadn't noticed it and couldn't see it now with the lights off. I had promised Danny to check in by ten. If I didn't, he was to call the police. Please, God, let it be past ten.

"Start the engine," Reeser said.

I could tell by the tone of his voice that he was beyond reason. When I didn't react fast enough, he poked my shoulder with straight hard fingers, starting another pulse of pain streaking down my arm. Somehow I got the truck running. The clock read 9:05.

"Now, drive," Reeser said.

TWENTY-FOUR

BACK OUT ON THE ROAD, Reeser's urgency was as palpable as the odor of his sweat. He was like a wild animal that feels the heat of the forest fire on his back, thinking of nothing but escaping the flames. Tamra returned to a wordless whimpering.

"The cops'll be back," I said. "Give it up, man. There aren't many roads up here, and damn little chance of getting away."

"Shut up," he said. "My head's pounding. And you," he gave Tamra a vicious shake. "Stop that goddamn noise. How can I think with the two of you at me like this?"

"We need to get off the road," I said. "Tamra and Lee are staying at a cabin—it's perfect. Way off the main drag. You could take something for your headache. Rest a few minutes."

Give Danny some time to call the police, a chance for them to piece it together.

"Oh, yeah," Reeser said. "Like you really give a shit about me."

"I care about all of us, Jerry. What happens when we pass another cop car? You can see I don't handle your truck so well. Next time we could go over a cliff."

"*No,*" he said. "You got some angle all figured out. You want me caught. You think I don't know that?"

"And you give me too much credit. I just want you

to have some time to clear your head and think before you get us all killed."

"Well, I'm not going to some fucking cabin, so forget it." His voice rose to an ugly crescendo, then it was quiet in the cab.

I had the chill sense that it was time to be silent for a while. Tamra had retreated someplace inside herself and was staring straight ahead. The night rushed by—endless trees and curving pavement. Another squad car howled past. This time Reeser said nothing.

We were coming up on the junction that could take us back to Route 18. Go that way and there should be more cars and more visibility if the authorities began looking for the truck. But there were also sheer drops off the Rim of the World Highway, and I imagined Reeser forcing me to race the police down that narrow, twisting stretch.

At the stop sign, Reeser gestured for me to turn right toward the village, then almost immediately said, "There," pointing to a sign that directed us left up a steep hill, bypassing the business center.

I had mixed feelings about being on Route 18, but I wasn't sure that this was better. I didn't know much about the roads up here. I was pretty sure, however, that there were a couple of routes that went through the mountains and ended up in the desert, and I could imagine those vast lonely stretches.

Tamra leaned against Reeser's shoulder as though she was too tired to hold her head up, but her eyes were fixed on the windshield, wide open, alive with fear in the reflection of the lights off the instrument panel. Reeser's never stopped moving. His gaze jumped from me to the road to the rearview mirror, back and forth.

We passed a few cars, but there was very little traffic. The feeling grew of being in our own private bubble, isolated from the night world outside the glass. The memory of sitting with Erik in the Lamborghini came to me, vivid and sensual, followed by a wrenching sense of loss, and I believed for the first time I might not get out of this one.

"Slow down," Reeser said.

Somehow the command scared me even worse. What was the alternative to flight? I soon found out.

"Stop!" he said. And then, "Back up."

A faint track went off into the forest, just two ruts in the bracken and weeds. Next to me I could feel Tamra tense and heard her draw in a shuddering breath. It was almost a quarter of ten. Another fifteen minutes before Danny would try to call me, even longer before he would call the police.

"Jerry," I said, "let's talk about this some more. Let's work it through."

"I know exactly what I'm doing," he said. "I was only in the bar for a few minutes. There wasn't much light in the parking lot. Nobody's going to remember me or the truck. But *you* know what happened—you and her."

"Jerry—"

"Get going. Move this fucking thing."

I shifted into first gear and turned off the pavement.

"It's your fault anyway," he said. "You and Lee—both of you. You wouldn't leave me alone. You just kept coming around, asking questions. And he kept calling me, threatening me."

Suddenly, I knew it all, the way it must have happened. I remembered the view from the Wylies' patio and from Tamra's room. You couldn't see into the Sannerman yard, but you could see the pasture, the barn, and the line of overgrown oleanders making the boundary fence.

"Lee saw you that day," I said. "He saw you leaving."

And I'd bet he went next door after he left Tamra's, maybe something in Reeser's movement alerting him. He must have found Kate's body there.

"She didn't want the neighbors to see me, so she always made me park down the hill and come up through the pasture," Reeser said. "I stayed close to the bushes. I thought I was safe."

"The gardeners saw a *car* parked at the foot of the hill," I said. "They didn't mention a truck."

"I got rid of the car. I traded it in. I was afraid somebody would recognize it."

So maybe that explained why the cops on the stakeout hadn't recognized the truck I'd described as belonging to Reeser.

The headlights sliced into the blackness, up and down as we bumped along the rough track, over rocks, dropping into unseen holes. Eyes glowed briefly, yellow and feral, some animal perched on a tree limb, watching as we passed.

"Lee introduced you to Kate," I said.

"One night in Rosita's," Reeser said. "I had some money. My father died a couple of years ago. I had his insurance. I was going to buy a condo. Lee said Kate could help me find one. She took me to look—and we—we were wonderful together, even that first day."

For several seconds he was silent, remembering the good times, I suppose. Then his face went stony.

"I never did buy the condo. The money's gone. I kept telling Lee that. I spent it on Kate. I'm in debt, for God's sake. And then she wouldn't see me anymore. That day—she laughed. She said she just needed me to buy the coke for her. *She said she never loved me.*"

The last was so anguished, I truly felt sorry for the guy.

"Jerry, you could make a jury understand that," I said. "I understand it. I do. She pushed you over the edge. You didn't plan to kill her."

"Stop the truck," he said.

"It wasn't premeditated. You'd go to jail for a while, but it wouldn't be forever—"

"Stop the fucking truck!" he screamed.

I braked, forgot the clutch. The engine stalled and died. The lights were still on, carving out a bright circle in front of us.

"Get out. You first." He shoved Tamra against me impatiently. "Open the door. *Now.*"

I did what he said, dropping down into knee-deep weeds. Tamra cried out as he pushed her ahead of him, retaining a grip on her arm.

I'm fairly sure I could have escaped then, run into the woods and been gone. God knows there was little chance he could have found me in the dark. Except, of course, I was sure he'd shoot Tamra if I ran, and I even had some remote hope that maybe if I stayed cool he would drive off and leave us there.

However, not being one to count on good fortune, I slipped my hand into my sweatshirt pocket. My fingers closed around the Beretta just as he shoved Tamra from the cab.

Maybe it was having her feet on solid ground again, maybe desperation overcame her near catatonia. Whatever triggered the action, he must have loosened his grip on her arm because Tamra yanked away from him and bolted. Even as his gun roared, I threw myself at Tamra and knocked her flat.

My ears rang with the explosion and my nose burned with the smell of cordite. Beneath me Tamra quivered and took great gulping breaths. I had no idea if she had been shot, but at least she was alive. But not for long, not either of us.

Reeser was half in, half out of the cab, the interior lights behind him, rendering him in faceless silhouette. We were in darkness. All night I'd been cursing the deep black nothingness created by the trees. Now I'm sure it was the very thing that saved us. Reeser hesitated because of it, and he couldn't see me take the Beretta from my pocket and thumb up the safety.

Any compunction I had about using the gun was long gone, all my interior debates forgotten.

His life for ours.

I never thought twice before I pulled the trigger.

TWENTY-FIVE

I DIDN'T KILL JERRY REESER, but not from lack of trying.

Although a .22 slug is small, it bounces around inside and causes a lot of damage. My bullet entered the abdominal cavity at an upward angle, nicked a couple of major organs, and wound up near Reeser's heart, requiring some tricky surgery to remove it.

So, while the bullet didn't kill him, it sure as hell stopped him, long enough for Tamra and me to get back in the truck and drive out of there. At the pavement I marked the rutted track, got to a phone, and summoned the police. A Medivac helicopter took Reeser out.

Lee had not been so lucky. He had died within minutes after being shot at close range. Aside from Tamra, there were very few people who mourned him.

Some weeks later I had a chance to talk to Jerry Reeser. As a matter of fact, he asked for me in the hospital, shortly before he was to be transferred to the Orange County Jail. When I arrived, he was sitting up in a chair, staring out the window. Since the view was of the parking lot and some scraggly palm trees, I thought he was really seeing something else, at least in his mind's eye.

He said a polite hello and invited me to pull up another chair and sit down as though it was a normal visit and I was a normal visitor instead of the person who put him there. He was very thin in the pale green hospital gown and robe. At forty-one his hair was going gray. Strangely, though, his face looked smoother now, almost unlined.

"How's Tamra Wylie?" he asked.

"Okay." Well, she wasn't quite all right just then, but I thought she would be. "You're satisfied with your PD?"

"Oh—yes. We haven't talked that much yet, but I'm sure he's fine."

"I have friends in the public defender's office, and I've heard good things about him."

After a few moments of awkward silence he said, "This is kind of weird, but I wanted you to know what really happened. You don't mind?"

"Not if it's okay with your attorney. I admit I'm surprised. Seems to me I'd be the last person you'd want to confide in."

He took a breath, steeling himself, I thought.

"That night in the mountains—I was a little crazy. I don't remember it all. I know you were saying anything you could to get me to stop, but when I told you about Kate, well, you said you understood. I thought you really seemed sincere, that you did know what I had gone through."

He paused, then went on quietly, with little emotion. All the while he was rubbing his thumb and forefinger back and forth on a seam in the robe. "I'm not trying to excuse myself, but I was under incredible pressure."

He was getting cocaine from Randy and Carlos for Kate, into them for a lot of money. The police knew. They put the squeeze on him too, promising to keep

him out of it when they busted the ring in return for
his cooperation. Meanwhile, things with Kate were
going to hell. He hadn't truly faced the fact that she
was using him until that last day.

"We were in the kitchen when she said—what she
said. The hammer was lying there on the counter. I
picked it up, and she laughed. She said I didn't have
the guts. She turned her back on me; walked outside.
I followed her and..."

I listened, any sympathy tempered with the memory of Kate's body left for the crows. I also wondered
if he was setting up some kind of defense here, hoping to use me to pull it off.

"Some people have bad luck—you notice that?" he
went on. "I do. I always have. So Lee was at the Wylies', and he saw me leave. He said Randy had told him
he'd cut me off. Lee had a little blow; he figured Kate
might need it. So he went over and found her. He said
he had helped me out, that he took money from her
purse to make it look like a robbery. Some friend."

A bitter smile thinned his lips.

"When you came to my office that first day, I almost left town. I wanted to just go away, to vanish. It
seemed like a miracle when Kate's husband was arrested. I thought if I could just get Lee off my
back... and then you left a message and when I
called—you know what you told me that day on the
phone? *I never give up.* I knew from the sound of your
voice it was true."

Randy didn't like me coming around either. A private cop was too close to the real thing. And the
stakeout team complained. None of them had any
suggestions about what to do with me. Mostly they

wanted to bitch. Then came Randy's call to tell him I
was back talking to Kevin, the call the cops had mentioned. Reeser decided to scare me off.

"That's all I meant to do," he said. "Seeing you
there in that parking lot at the mall—I think that's
when I went over the edge, really over. The next day,
mostly it was like everything was happening to somebody else. Trying to get the windshield fixed, then Lee,
and you—there again with Tamra Wylie..."

"In the middle of all this, did you ever consider
Robb Sannerman?" I asked. "How he was in jail for
a murder you committed?"

"I like to think that I would have said something—
maybe—but I don't know, I just don't know—" He
stood up abruptly and said, "Well, I won't take any
more of your time. Thank you for coming."

I saw his hand then. The skin on his thumb and
forefinger was raw, and there was blood on the seam
of the robe, but he seemed completely unaware of it.

At the door he said, "What you did, shooting me,
it was really for the best. Remember that—whatever
happens."

He died that night. They found him at the morning
shift change. He'd broken the mirror in the bathroom
and used the shards to cut his wrists.

AFTER REESER'S ARREST, the cops had to abort the
surveillance down at the Hilltop Apartments. None of
the guys in 19D were charged; they got immunity for
cooperating with the police. Rosita's was raided, and
a major drug bust took place up in Garden Grove.
Newspaper reports put the street value of the cocaine
at $20 million.

No attorney was necessary to get Kevin Ross out of his lease, a couple of well-placed phone calls did the trick. Randy and his pals were served an eviction notice.

As for Tamra, Ben and Marilyn Wylie blame each other for what happened, but, to their credit, they worked together long enough to help Tamra over the trauma. Neither liked it much, however, when they realized their daughter had done a lot of growing up that night in the mountains. They especially didn't like it because some kind of bond had been forged between Tamra and me, and Tamra decided I was a perfect role model. Well, I didn't blame the Wylies a whole lot for being upset over that one.

Bullheaded as ever—genes will tell—Tamra didn't believe all the bad stuff about Lee until she heard it from enough people to convince her. One of the people she talked to was Kevin. She talked to him a lot. Determined to become the independent and decisive woman she thought me to be, she decided the first step was to leave home. Since Kevin needed a roommate, she moved in with him. And they both decided to stay at Hilltop. It was handy to college and to work. Tamra signed up for a full load of classes and landed a job at the Italian restaurant which had replaced Rosita's.

Meanwhile, Randy and company were fighting the eviction and lying low, especially after Tamra and Kevin took some self-defense classes, and, one memorable night, Tamra felled big bad Bix with one well-placed karate chop.

Robb tried to sell the house in Nellie Gail, but the housing market was rotten, not to mention the problem of selling a place where a gruesome murder had occurred. The bank finally foreclosed. After paying Leah Bennett and me, he used the rest of Kate's insurance money to move to Florida to be with his mother and help her take care of his father.

Now, about Erik...

UP AT ARROWHEAD I had insisted Tamra be taken to the emergency room of the small local hospital. There was nothing physically wrong with her, but the doctor thought she ought to be sedated and kept overnight.

Of course I got an earful from Benjamin Wylie later, but at least I didn't have to deal with him right then. The sheriff's department and the hospital did that.

It was just after midnight when the police finally agreed to let me leave and come back the next day for a formal statement. I had, after all, shot Reeser in self-defense and in so doing had helped them nab Lee Gersky's killer. Otherwise, all I'd done was break a few laws regarding local firearms ordinances.

I called Erik from the van at the scenic overlook along the Rim of the World Highway.

"I'm sorry," I said. "Did I wake you up?"

"Delilah? No, I couldn't sleep. What is it? Are you all right?"

"I'm just leaving Lake Arrowhead. No questions, okay? I know it's awfully late, but can I come see you?"

"Of course," he said. "I'll wait up."

Except for construction, at that hour the freeways were operating the way they were designed to work. I made it to the coast in record time. Just north of Laguna Beach I turned off PCH onto a narrow asphalt road and drove up through wisps of fog that drifted above the dry chaparral and sandstone boulders of the coastal hills. Up ahead, at a high stone wall that had been carefully hidden with landscaping, the guard saw me coming and opened the gate so I didn't even have to slow down.

I parked in front of the huge mission-style house at the top of the hill. The house was mostly dark except for the entry lights, all brightly lit.

Erik met me at the door as though he'd been standing there waiting since I called. More likely the guard had alerted him. He was wearing a ratty old L.L. Bean cotton sweater and dark blue sweatpants and looking tired and worried. I saw both consternation and relief in his eyes. Well, my clothes were dirty and Lord knows what my face and hair looked like, but at least I was in one piece.

"God, I was worried about you," he said. "Let's go sit down and you can tell me what happened. Do you want some brandy? Are you hurt?"

"I didn't come to talk," I said.

Ever since I'd left Arrowhead I'd felt as though some unrelenting force had been driving me straight here. But at that moment, truth is, I almost turned and fled. Instead I said, "Come on," and led the way down a hall to some double doors in the back. I'd been there only once, but I remembered, all right. Erik had taken me to his bedroom suite the night we met to show me the three Monet paintings on the walls of the sitting room.

I went past the artwork into the room beyond. The covers had been turned down, but the king-size bed hadn't been slept in. The drapes were drawn to reveal a sliding glass door that opened onto a balcony. I caught a glimmer of lights through the fog, curving along the dark sweep of the Pacific.

I took off my zippered sweatshirt and tossed it on the floor, saying, ''We both know what's going on between us—chemistry—all those pheromones, or whatever the damn things are flying around.''

I tried to unbutton the sleeves of my shirt and couldn't do it. I was shaking, either from excitement or a delayed reaction, probably both. ''Help me here, will you?'' I held out my arm.

''I mean, of course it's never going to work,'' I said while he undid the buttons and slid the shirt off my shoulders. ''We have absolutely nothing in common.''

I pulled the tank top off, then managed the buttons on my slacks okay—and the zipper. The loose trousers fell down around my ankles and I kicked them off, revealing that my left leg was almost as colorful with bruises as the right.

I heard Erik's quick intake of breath.

''Okay, so I lied about last night,'' I said. ''Some guy tried to kill me. He tried again a few hours ago. This time I was really afraid he was going to do it too. And you know what I was thinking? That I was going to die and that you and I were never going to make love.''

''Ah, sweetheart,'' he said and drew me into his arms.

From the feel of his body and the way he kissed me I knew that making love to Erik was not something I was going to miss out on.

AFTER ROBB WAS RELEASED and I got the business with the Arrowhead police settled, Erik and I flew up to San Francisco for a long weekend. In his private jet, of course. At the Intercontinental, penthouse suite. Although I don't know why we bothered. We never left the hotel.

I told myself that it was the right thing to do, what I should have done months ago. A wild, crazy fling, like the fever you have with the flu, all-consuming until it finally burns itself out. I'd get Erik out of my system and get on with my life.

Sounded good. Sounded right.

One problem.

I'm not sure it's working.

EVENTUALLY, the San Bernardino Sheriff's Department returned my small arsenal. I had plenty of time to brood about handguns and violence. And every time I opened the paper, I saw some new tidbit. For instance: there are now almost two hundred million guns owned by private citizens in the United States— enough so every man, woman, and child above the age of five can have his own. And: in Orange County homicides doubled in the last ten years; deaths by gunshot jumped 52 percent. Carjackings and drive-by shootings account for a big portion of the increase; home invasions are coming on strong.

We live in a dangerous world. Nobody can deny it, me least of all. Still, I have to wonder and never mind that Reeser had exonerated me. If I hadn't bought the Beretta, if I hadn't tucked it in my pocket and taken it along that night, would I have found another way to deal with Jerry Reeser? Knowing I had the weapon, had I relied on it rather than on my powers of persuasion?

I try to remember clearly: the noise when Reeser fires, the smell of cordite, the cold certainty that in a very few seconds he'd pull the trigger and another round will tear into my body and Tamra's.

I conclude that I hate the idea of violence as much as ever, but that I'm damn glad I had the means to defend myself.

I'll keep the guns.

The Lost Keats

Terence Faherty

First Time in Paperback

An Owen Keane Mystery

FROM KEATS TO A KILLER...

A man with more questions than answers, Owen Keane has one foot in the priesthood, the other in detective novels—a trait that finds him questioning his own vocation. So when a fellow seminarian disappears, Owen sees it as a chance to unravel a mystery, and perhaps his own inner struggles.

But it's not until he meets a descendant of the English poet John Keats that scattered clues fall into place. At the center is a missing sonnet, but from there things turn modern—with marijuana and murder adding to the mystery that becomes deadly as Owen gets closer to the truth...and to a killer with a message just for him.

"A near-faultless performance." —*Publishers Weekly*

Available in February at your favorite retail stores.

To order your copy, please send your name, address, zip or postal code along with a check or money order (please do not send cash) for $5.50 for each book ordered ($5.99 in Canada), plus 75¢ postage and handling ($1.00 in Canada), payable to Worldwide Mystery, to:

In the U.S.	In Canada
Worldwide Mystery	Worldwide Mystery
3010 Walden Avenue	P. O. Box 609
P. O. Box 1325	Fort Erie, Ontario
Buffalo, NY 14269-1325	L2A 5X3

Please specify book title with your order.
Canadian residents add applicable federal and provincial taxes.

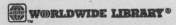 **WORLDWIDE LIBRARY®**

KEATS

Take 3 books and a surprise gift FREE

SPECIAL LIMITED-TIME OFFER

Mail to: The Mystery Library™
3010 Walden Ave.
P.O. Box 1867
Buffalo, N.Y. 14269-1867

YES! Please send me 3 free books from the Mystery Library™ and my free surprise gift. Then send me 3 mystery books, first time in paperback, every month. Bill me only $3.69 per book plus 25¢ delivery and applicable sales tax, if any*. There is no minimum number of books I must purchase. I can always return a shipment at your expense and cancel my subscription. Even if I never buy another book from the Mystery Library™, the 3 free books and surprise gift are mine to keep forever.   415 BPY ANQ2

Name	(PLEASE PRINT)

Address	Apt. No.

City	State	Zip

KINDNESS CAN KILL
JANIE BOLITHO

First Time in Paperback

An Inspector Ian Roper Mystery

NOT A PRETTY PICTURE

Stunningly beautiful, brazenly sexy, Julia Henderson was every man's fantasy and every wife's nightmare—until her brutal murder rocks the quiet English village of Rickenham Green.

Detective Chief Inspector Ian Roper and his team sort out the clues and conclude this was no illicit one-nighter gone insane. It was deliberate and emotional. Whoever killed Julia knew her well.

So twisted are the sins and secrets of some community members that two will confess to killing Julia. But it's the identity of her true killer that remains as shocking as it is inevitable.

"Taut, psychologically compelling..."   *—Publishers Weekly*

Available in February at your favorite retail stores.

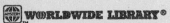

A RECONSTRUCTED CORPSE

SIMON BRETT

A Charles Paris Mystery

First Time in Paperback

A STIFF ACT TO FOLLOW...

If playing a dead man could be called a role, Charles Paris has sunk to new lows when he agrees to play missing Martin Earnshaw on the true crime TV series "Public Enemies."

The show has all the hallmarks of a hit: a vulnerable, tearful wife, a sexy female detective and, best of all, dismembered limbs probably belonging to Earnshaw turning up each week just before airtime.

As viewers shudder gleefully and ratings soar, Paris discovers there's more to the whole production than meets the eye…and the climax is a killer.

"A perfect vacation read."   *—People*

Available in March at your favorite retail stores.